They are different
Mike

Possibilities

Exodus and Other Stories

Mike Furst

PublishAmerica
Baltimore

First printing

ISBN: 1-4241-6163-0
PUBLISHED BY PUBLISHAMERICA, LLLP
www.publishamerica.com
Baltimore

Printed in the United States of America

Acknowledgments

These stories are the work of my imagination and personal experiences. I have had encouragement along the way by both friends and family, who have made suggestions and sometimes commented on the writing itself.

My wife has shown me things that made me think more deeply about my life experiences, and I have used this in some of my writing.

More recently I have been privileged to watch grandchildren become thinking beings. This and my computer background have influenced my thinking on artificial intelligence, and I have tried to explore this in my writing.

Three of these stories have been written because of my thinking about people close to me who have died.

I thank all these people, friends and family, who have influenced my life and contributed to my story writing.

—Mike Furst

Possibilities: Exodus and Other Stories

I hope these stories will entertain you. If they fire your imagination, please share them with a child. Their future will require imagination and a sense of humor. I can't imagine a future without laughter.

—Mike Furst, Summer 2005

Table of Contents

EXODUS 11
This is the beginning of our story. This is how we were forced to flee our Homeworld and become wanderers in search of a place where we could start life anew.

HERITAGE 55
Of course when they came in their scout vehicles, we welcomed them. But when we wouldn't do everything they wanted, they turned their weapons on us. What did we know about war?

SATURDAY NIGHT 66
I guess I'm a map person. Some people I know have never looked at a map, but when I look I see many different ways to get to where I'm going besides the heavy lines—as a great American poet once said, "the road less traveled by." One of my best adventures was when I did follow a thin wavy line.

CHILD 72
Al knew that he was still a Child—the first of its kind. And as all children do, he wondered what he would become when he grew up.

MAGIC VILLAGE 97
"A child sees the world through the eyes of a child. With maturity comes a more worldly view."

THE CLUB 107
There have always been secret societies dedicated to strange endeavors. Almost always the price of memberships involves some sort of initiation, and of course, one must be invited to become a member. I cannot say more without revealing too much, but I will say that there exists a secret society known simply as...THE CLUB

FLASHBACKS! 112
I'll tell you about flashbacks. I keep mine in a box in the back of the closet underneath a pile of old clothes. The box has a lock on it, but every once in a while, in the early hours of the morning, I swear the sound of the lid opening wakes me, and then...

A SMALL TOWN IN IOWA 114
A town so small that even on a cloudless day, it really couldn't be seen from orbit.

ONE PHOTON 120
Imagine, if you can, being in a losing battle and wishing to run away so far that you would never be found. Now imagine that your wish came true.

THE GIFT 123
Children, of course, are the greatest gift of all. Out of love, we give them to ourselves.

RAIN 125
It is good for many things—flowers, trees, and growing boys.

ENDNOTES 133

EXODUS

Of course when they came in their scout vehicles; we welcomed them. But when we wouldn't do everything they wanted, they turned their weapons on us. What did we know about war? We never fought anyone; it's not in our genes! We did the only thing we could; we hid. And when that didn't work, we scattered. Some of us made it out to space—to the stars. Of course, I can never know about the others, my cousins and parents. I only can chronicle how we ran and hid.

Excerpt from jon rmlagas early chronicles. In the beginning his name was not capitalized. Even at the end he refused to capitalize his name, thinking that he was not worthy. Great leaders and revered groups, of course, are capitalized to show respect.

EXODUS—this is the beginning of our story. This is how we were forced to flee our Homeworld and become wanderers in search of a place where we could start life anew.

In the beginning

They commanded us to build an ark populated with representational plants and animals to be shipped to their world as part of a museum. We never doubted that some of us would become part of the display; according to *them* we are all animals.

In the ark

For me it was a challenge to say this just right to our captain. How could I tell him that we all had faith in his leadership, but we now had an opportunity to save the crew of the returning explorer ship Newhope, and also acquire its captain, a person of great achievement and world acclaim? It would be an honor to have him, along with all of his select crew. All of their additional talents would help our survival.

The explorer ship, Newhope, had left Homeworld two solar revolutions ago, captained by Anon, the leading space explorer and renowned scientist, along with a hand-picked crew. They were on their way home with the results of their exploration of three of our eight planets. They could not know of the events on Homeworld, which had made us subject to the whims of *them*, our conquerors. If we could only tell him what had happened and give Captain Anon and his crew a chance to join us before they were captured by Homeworld. I came up with a plan; it was simple, but I thought it would work. To this end, I arranged a seemingly chance encounter with our captain in order to present my case.

Seeing the captain approaching the mainroom, I established myself directly in his path and concentrated on a small notepad that I was holding.

"Captain Narlo, I am so sorry. I should not have been blocking the doorway," I said, just after we had collided.

"No harm done."

I continued to look at him, not quite knowing what next to do. He seemed to sense that I had something to say and looked at me questioningly. I judged it best to just launch into what I wanted to ask him, so I said, "So, Captain, since we are in orbit, we have a clear shot at the returning explorer. We should be able to flash a laser at them to get their attention before they are seen from below. Then we can tell them to stay quiet and land backside of our second moon. We can rendezvous with them using our shuttle and get them on board without being noticed from below. We need to get fuel from that moon anyway and we can get them here on a fuel run."

The captain bought the idea. I had the feeling that he needed someone to share his duties. Piloting a ship to nowhere is an awesome responsibility, sure to take years off his life.

He said, "Anon is a good man, and I know many of the crew personally. It would be good to have them aboard. I also know that they would not want to live as they would be forced to, once they returned to Homeworld."

I said nothing, but I thought of the implications. They would be guarded and considered useful pets by *them.* No real person could tolerate this for long.

"Okay, jon. Set up a red laser under guidance control pointing to their probable position, assuming that they are on the shortest course home from the last planet that they explored. That beam would not be visible except to the Newhope, unless they have company. Keep the power low; they will see it long before we or Homeworld can see them."

The captain thought a moment. I was about to say more, but he held up his hand to stop me. After a time, he said, "Use a standard emergency beacon. Have it say, *Batson building auditorium.*"

Now I was confused. "But captain, why that message?

"Just do it. Believe me; they will know what it means better than anything else you can say."

"Okay," I said. "Are you sure that they will know we need to communicate in secret?"

The captain nodded a yes, so I turned and walked away.

When the captain had regained his privacy, he started to grin, and the grin turned into a soft but audible chuckle. He was remembering the time in advanced pilot training when he and his classmates plotted to remove the statue of the founder and replace it with that of an armoorer, the dumbest animal known; not even good to eat. They had gone around all week with their red directional night lights, taping out instructions to each other so no one else could see. Their final meeting was in the *Batson building auditorium.* Their escapade had worked, and they volunteered to replace the statue, which was "found" the next day in the cafeteria. It would not have worked had they not used the directional secure signaling between them. At least four of his classmates were on the crew of the returning ship, and they would know what the message meant.

It was a simple task to compute the trajectory of the returning explorers. The real problem would be how to know where along that trajectory they would be. Jon finally decided that he would use several lasers and aim them at his best guess location and a few days ahead and behind. He also knew that the signal could be seen just a bit off axis, so he was reasonably sure that he had everything covered. He found an inertially stabilized construction platform that was exactly right. Since all equipment had an emergency beacon, all he had to do was add two more, set up the special directions to each of the beacons, and use a construction arm to set it in place outside the ark. Although the task was simple, it had still taken the better part of a ship's day, and it was now well into ship's night. He would wait until the morning to tell the captain.

The next morning, jon awoke to the sound of a message request. He turned off the beep and read the screen. It read, "The captain wishes to see you immediately."

Donning fresh ship's clothes and making a quick bathroom stop, he presented himself at the captain's quarters where he was immediately summoned in.

"Jon, they received our message and understood it. The answer arrived an hour ago."

"What did they say?"

"Green snot?"

"What?" I asked.

"I can understand your confusion, jon. They were asking who sent the message. I, of course, replied with, 'Fifthday meal,' which they acknowledged with one short flash."

"I still don't get it," I said.

"Well, that's because you were never at the academy. The first message was a building that we were all familiar with and involved secure communications. Their response was the name we gave to the Fifthday meal where several of us got sick. Only those who were there would know the correct answer."

As I began to understand what had just happened, I found myself thinking that our captain was also in that elite group that was well beyond the average. We were lucky to have him, too.

"Jon," the captain continued, "I will set up the details of getting them on board. Because we have two short messages from them, we know their trajectory and can now point directly at them, assuring privacy. Your plan was a good one, and we got them just in time because they were about to send a message home informing them of their arrival. For now, tell no one lest word get out."

True to his word, the captain arranged for them to get on board.

We were still in the dark about what was going on, but arrangements were made for us to meet on moon two, far side. The captain was kind enough to include me in the party. We took a shuttle with an attached cargo pod to pick up fuel, but hopefully to pick up the returning crew. We were descending to the surface when the captain turned on the emergency beacon. "Look for a single flash from the surface," the captain said.

About two minutes later, we all saw a single red flash, off to the right, not very far away. Immediately we went into a tight right spiral; the captain would do a manual landing almost on top of where the flash came from.

It then came together for me. The low-power emergency beacon would be seen from the ground, and a very directional flash would indicate their location, with minimal risk of anyone else observing our rendezvous. Our descent was made under radar guidance using manual control. Radar was required because being on the darkside eliminated most visual clues. However, our final approach was made using red light. Just before touchdown, the captain rotated us so we could see the explorer ship from the front window. Although we had all seen pictures of the departure two years ago, what I was looking at now was not much larger than our own shuttlecraft.

The captain turned off power and said, "In case you are wondering why it looks so much smaller, it is because they discarded ship sections as fuel and supplies were used. Even now they have a section that they could discard, so they have more than what they needed for the return."

That was all he said at the time, being a man of few words, but he did point to his helmet indicating that we all should put ours on, which we did. He then inspected each of us, and only then did he depressurize and open the hatch.

As we emerged, we saw a single space-suited figure, waving his arm to indicate that we should enter the explorer, Newhope, or what was left of it. Our captain was the first on the surface and proceeded directly to the Newhope. The rest of us, of course, followed, and entered the hatch. Although the inside felt bigger than it looked from the outside, it could by no means be described as roomy or luxurious. As soon as the ship was sealed and pressurized, our captain took off his helmet and was recognized by several of the seated crew and a standing figure whose insignia indicated that he was captain Anon. Their crew was greatly animated; joyful would be a good way to describe it, as they had not seen anybody but themselves for two years. Both captains made asalam, the hand to shoulder touch that was both a formal greeting and friendly acknowledgment.

Anon, the captain of the Newhope, was the first to speak. "Narlo, it is so good to see you, although I never expected these circumstances."

"It is good to see you, Anon, under any circumstances. I wish that they were different."

Both captains stared at each other for what seemed like a very long time. Finally Anon spoke. "Does this have anything to do with the alien contact that was happening shortly after we left?"

"It has everything to do with it."

"Then it's true," said Anon.

"We have been monitoring the networks from Homeworld on the way in. We did not know what to make of it. Has our entire race been subjugated to *them*? What is really going on?"

It was then that captain Narlo explained what had happened. Everyone stood or sat silently, listening to every word. He did not paint a pretty picture. The control of our citizens for their purposes was shameful, and yet we had succumbed easily. He explained that when we had opposed *them* we were killed or subjected to other forms of coercion.

And finally, he came to why we were all here now. That we had built the ark for their zoo, supplied specimens from our Homeworld, and most likely ourselves included.

I could see Anon thinking. His face grew more serious. It seemed that he was following Narlos' thoughts and also forming his own at the same time.

Narlo paused, looking at Anon. "Well, I can see that the ark is a ready-made escape vehicle, and clearly it is possible. I think, though, that my crew and I should discuss this before we say we will join you."

We all looked at each other, and the Newhope crew looked at captain Anon. They each gestured yes. Then captain Anon looked at each of them and called them by name. Each, in turn, said aloud, "I'm in, Captain."

"Well, then, it looks like that is it. I'll need my crew until we are done with what's left of the Newhope; this old ship has a few things to contribute."

"Done!" said our captain Narlo.

And with that we all made asalam, introduced each other, and spoke about what had happened in the last two years in general and personally. Somehow, food appeared, as did tables with seating for all of us. Our captain reached into a pocket on his suit and brought out an odd-shaped bottle. It had a leaf shape with engraved details, but a leaf that I, for one, had never seen before.

"People," said our captain. "This bottle contains a special extract made by the interactions of a plant and a beetle. The plant has a leaf like the bottle, and it is found in secret places known only to the manufacturer. It is very rare, and quite potent, so each of us will get just enough so that it will go around. Some vessels, please."

A crewmember reached into a locker, brought out a stack of small drink containers, and passed them to our captain. Now our captain did a remarkable thing; it may have been a small thing, but I thought of it as a sign that all would go well on our mutual adventure. What he did was, without counting, extract a stack of containers, place them on the table and filled each of them to the same level. When he filled the last container, he had consumed all of the liquid and not once did he go back to adjust the level in any of them. Then he said, "Drink up. To our voyage."

Each of us took a vessel and there were just enough for everyone, no more and no less. The taste was beyond description. When we spoke of it later, each of us tasted something different and yet wonderful. It gave us an immediate sense of well-being and made us feel that we were surrounded by long-time friends. The effect lasted long after we had said our short goodbye and retired to our own craft for night sleep.

We awoke to the sounds of the shuttle powering up for takeoff. Our captain told us to just check our security straps, but nothing dramatic was expected. It would be several hours before we would be back to the ark, and we would use this time to talk about what we would do next. Captain Narlo did not engage in any of this conversation, but would only say that there was a plan and not to say anything about what happened to anyone.

The next several days were stressful to all of us who went on that last shuttle flight. We could not talk about it lest we be overheard, yet we felt that there were things that we could do. In fact, weren't there things that we should do?

I started to notice little changes that I guessed were part of the plan. The first thing was that when I looked out at Homeworld, it was smaller. Somehow we were in a higher orbit, and yet we were circling Homeworld faster. Also, the last up shipments did not contain any animals, but rather a large and varied vegetable selection, all of which were edible. And for some reason, they were all ripe and bearing viable seeds. Then, two sevendays after our rendezvous, an announcement came over ship's sound. "Attention everyone; this is Captain Narlo speaking. We will be checking our engines by taking a flight around second moon. This has been cleared below, and a course correction will be made within the hour. The ark is not made for rapid maneuvers, so you will not feel more than one-tenth gravity. Since this is a change from weightlessness, you will fall to the deck. I will orient the ark so that the deck will be down. When we pass behind the moon, all communications with

Homeworld will be temporarily lost. Please finish any work with them in the next five minutes."

True to his word, five minutes later we were behind the moon. A minute later, a loud bang was heard. Looking through the view port, I did not see us speeding across the moon surface, but our path was such that the moon continued to block out Homeworld. I did not know what was happening, but clearly the captain had planned this carefully. I also felt heavier. I had an idea of what was happening but I needed to make sure, so I went to the loading area and looked out the small viewport. Because the loading area was in the lower part of the ark, I could see the aft end of our craft. My guess was confirmed! There was the Newhope explorer attached to our ship and with its main engine on. Our four outboard engines were also on, but at far reduced power.

We traveled this way for the next sevenday, keeping the moon almost fully between Homeworld and us while our speed was increasing dramatically. Our captain was giving status reports at every shift change, saying that the trial was going well, and we could be proud. When the ship's engines were shut, we all felt an immediate weight loss, but not the zero gravity that we were expecting. Again, I made a trip to the loading area and saw that the Newhope still had its engine on. We were being pushed and were still accelerating. Although I knew that Homeworld would be a bright planet at this distance, I could not see it from this view port. I was really confused, and I started towards the control center to confront our captain. At that moment, from ship's sound, a major chord was followed by, "The captain requests that we all meet in the main room in five minutes. Please be there."

If the sudden change in gravity wasn't enough to get everyone's attention, the appearance of the explorer crew walking towards the mainroom was the topper. As we all crowded into the room, our conversations became subdued, and we cleared a path for the strangers to walk to the stage where the captain was waiting. It did not take long for Captain Anon to be recognized along with his crew. Word of who they were spread quickly. When our captain gestured that we should sit on the empty floor, we all sat down and quieted in anticipation that all would be made clear.

Captain Narlo raised both of his hands in the customary gesture indicating that he had the lead. He started, "When you all became part of the company working on the ark, you only knew that you were being coerced into the job and had little choice. Since then, you, me, all of us have become an extended family, working together and caring about each other. As for myself, I find that even as I am one of you, because I am the captain, I am the one responsible for the well-being of each of us, and collectively, all of us.

"As our home, the ark, took shape, it became apparent that it could sustain us all for a long time. Also, the conditions on Homeworld are not good, and there does not seem to be much that we can do about it. However, there have been ongoing discussions about starting anew on some as-yet-uncharted planet and using this ark as an escape vehicle. Therefore, we have been provisioning ourselves with edible plants, some animals, and seeds to grow our food using soil that we loaded for fuel. Not that the soil would burn, but our atomic power plant generates thrust by accelerating material to fractional light speed. Anything having mass would do.

"Jon, who I see seated at the far left, brought to my attention that the explorer ship Newhope was returning from its long trip, and that we could bring them aboard, if we did it so that Homeworld does not suspect. That you see here Captain Anon and his crew, attests to our success in doing just that. Besides planetary knowledge that they have acquired, they bring a remarkable array of talents and skills that we will need if we are to be successful in our journey.

"As you may have guessed, we are not in orbit around Homeworld any more, and in fact we are well on our way to whatever the fates have set out for us."

With that, there was a great clamor from all assembled. Very few had guessed what was happening, and all wanted to add their voices to the conversations taking place.

"Captain, how do we know that we are not being pursued? Are we to be hunted down and killed?"

"We discussed this at great length. I do not have an answer to that question, but I can tell you that we did everything possible to avoid it. First, we never told anyone our plans, lest someone give it away. Next, we covered up our escape by faking a test run around second moon. And, at Captain Anon's suggestion, just before communications were blanked as we went behind the moon, we signaled frantically that our control jets had malfunctioned, and we would attempt a moon landing to fix them.

"What you did not know was that the Newhope explorer had attached itself to us and was adding its thrust to help our escape. All the while, we had been keeping the moon between Homeworld and us so that all would think we had either crashed or landed on the backside of the moon. This, we think, bought us some time. Even now we are accelerating using the explorers' engine only, since if we used ours also, the ionization trail would more easily be noticed."

There was much discussion among the crowd. I waited for the question that I knew would be coming. I did not have to wait long. It came from someone way in the back of the room.

"Captain Narlo, we were not asked if we wanted to go on this adventure. Some of us have families expecting us back. We have loved ones who we did not have a chance to say goodbye to. What about us?"

Captain Anon stepped forward and raised both his hands. "I'll answer that," he said.

"Captain Narlo and I discussed giving people a way to opt out, but the risk of compromising secrecy was unacceptable. We had to make a decision, and we did. Captain Narlo also suggested that we make the explorer available as a return ship for those requesting it. I refused to allow my ship to be used that way because it is too valuable to our mission. It contains equipment that we will need to find a suitable planet for us. It also contains an advanced computer that we have used to get us out of a few bad situations, and, we have loaded it up with soil to be used as fuel or for anything else."

He then looked around the room, meeting each and everyone's gaze. Not one protest was heard. I was impressed! There is much to be said for group solidarity.

Almost as if it were planned, as Captain Anon stepped back, we were suddenly back to weightlessness. This time Captain Narlo floated forward with outstretched arms.

"People, our initial powered phase has just terminated. We are no longer occluded by moon two, and we can be seen from Homeworld if they know where to look. If you look out a viewport, Homeworld can be seen as the bright object in the sky.

"I suggest that you arrange your laboratories and quarters for weightlessness, as this will be our state until further notice. Thank you for your solidarity. We all have much work to do."

And with that, both captains and the crew left the room. I left the room, too, because, as was just said, there was much work to be done.

We all sensed that something was wrong when the background ship's sound system switched from the normal control room chatter to soothing music. I was speaking with Dhalyiska, our leading religious spokesperson, recruited from the backcountry of Nevron. Well, he was more rescued than recruited, since his entire village was being held hostage to force us to mine bromadulim jewels for their pleasure.

He was saying to me, "Jon, I know that something is dreadfully wrong. I sense it."

I looked at him intently. There was something about him that indicated, to me at least, that he was an extraordinary individual. His mind was always inquiring about anything he saw, and his conversations always showed a great depth of understanding and sensitivity for other viewpoints.

"Dhal," I said, having gotten familiar enough with him so that I could call him by his shortened name.

"The sudden change in ship's sound has gotten everyone nervous. It usually is a prelude to an announcement of something. The last time it was a course change, and the time before that is was long-term food rationing."

"I remember," Dhal said, "but if nothing happens soon, I will go to the command center and ask what is going on."

Just then, the music stopped, to be replaced by the captain's voice. "This is the captain speaking. Something of great importance has happened on Homeworld. Rather than tell you myself, I will replay a broadcast by *them*, which we have just received. Of course, it has been delayed one-eighth day because that is our light distance from home. Please sit down and clear your mind."

Silence; no one said anything. The loudest sound was the air circulation system—and our collective breathing.

Then, "Hear this, you weaklings! You had been commanded to build a space ark and populate it with specimens of your world. Some time ago we saw this ark disappear from orbit, departing for parts unknown. You will build another one as we command. Rather than waste time hunting down the fleeing ark, we have chosen to make an example for you to see our power and obey our wishes. Consequently, your city that you call Hope will cease to exist in fifteen minutes. Do as you wish, but at that time the city will be destroyed. Work on the new ark will start in five days, after you attend to your dead."

Short pause. "This is your captain again. We have been monitoring spectral emission from our planet and have just seen a strong line in the hydrogen band. This occurred exactly fifteen minutes after we received the broadcast that you just heard. It lasted twenty seconds and is indicative of extremely intense energy. We believe that they have carried out their threat."

Again, silence. And then, softly at first, the sound of crying.

It was a strange sound to us. None of us had ever heard more than one or two adults cry at the same time, and yet here there were hundreds.

From the ship's sound, in the captain's voice, "We will meet in the mainroom in one hour. Prepare yourself to share whatever thoughts you may have on this."

Dhal looked at me and said, "Friend jon, I feel that there are things that I must say. I go now to be alone and harvest my thoughts."

We gathered in the mainroom well before the hour was up. Most of us touched each other in passing and nodded acknowledgment of our mutual grief.

I looked at Dhal. He looked at peace somehow. When it came his turn, he rose slowly and made eye contact with those present. Then slowly and with great feeling he said, "Our grief is so great that it cannot be expunged. We shall be forever cursed with guilt unless we accept that which we do not understand as somehow part of the grand plan. Now is the time not to curse God, but to say that all sentient beings have free will and can do terrible things as we have just witnessed. We can hope that the future will bring a true kingdom of the Creator with peace for all sentient beings.

"Therefore, let us accept that we are all part of God's plan. And for ourselves, let us reaffirm our faith."

And then, in a voice so low that we all strained to hear each word, he began to sing.

Let us sanctify God's great name in the universe which He created according to His will.
May he establish His kingdom during our lifetime and during the lifetime of our people. So be it!
May God's great name be blessed forever and ever.
Although God is beyond all praises and songs of adoration that can be uttered, let us say, So be it!
May there be peace and life for all of us and for all our people. Let us say, So be it!
Let He who makes peace in the heavens, grant peace to all of us here and to all our kind. So be it!
And Let this be so.

When he was done, there was a noise from the far right; it was from shema, who appeared extremely agitated. I remembered that shema was hatched in a mining camp where at the age of eight, he was the sole survivor of an explosion. He was taken to Hope City, where he was accepted into a new extended family and raised to adulthood. This would be the second time that he had been the sole survivor where all of his family was killed.

Shema cried out in despair. "You cannot foul our planet without answering to God! There is only one God."

And then he continued, "Is not the one God their God also? Do they not have a responsibility to our God? Will not our God, who is slow to anger, show his wrath to them?"

He rested a moment, as if to gather is thoughts. We all became very still, not knowing what he would say next, but all knowing that whatever he would say would be important.

Then, he gathered himself to his full height, extended his hand, pointing to the heavens, and in a loud voice full of rage, he cried out, "Hear every living being! The Lord is our God; the Lord is the One God!"

These words, a plea for God to do something and uttered in despair, somehow resonated within all of us. Silence followed shema's last sentence. Then, softly, a voice was heard. "So be it."

And then, another, "So be it."

And then another and another, until all of us had echoed the traditional "So be it," that was used to show agreement and to honor what was said.

Although we could not know it at the time, Dahl's words to reaffirm our faith at the loss of our loved ones would become part of our heritage, as would shema's defiant exhortation.

We left the gathering, if not with spirits raised, then at least with guarded optimism about the future.

Two arkdays later

"Narlo, take a walk with me to the explorer," said Anon.

Captain Narlo stretched to full length and then pushed towards Captain Anon, matching his zero-gravity drift. They made their way through the double hatches into the smaller explorer. Captain Anon pushed the hatch almost shut.

"Narlo," he said, "I feel uneasy about *them.* I know that in their broadcast they said that they would not pursue us, but that does not mean that they won't. Perhaps they said that so we would be off guard. Soon we must decide where we are going and make a course correction. At that time, if they are looking, they will see our exhaust energy. Your thoughts?"

Narlo smiled, looked directly at Anon and said, "Friend Anon, this is just like at school. You read my thoughts. I too, have been uneasy. More than uneasy, because what we do affects all our lives. You were always better at taking responsibility for others than I, and I now tell you that I am glad to be able to share this command."

They both seemed to be waiting for the other to say something. Finally Anon said, "Let us get some informed thoughts. Can you ask others to join us?"

"I have two in mind. One is a generalist who has done much for us, and another is expert in psychology and religion. I respect his wisdom on many subjects."

He keyed the intercom, "Jon rmlagas and Dhalyiska please report to the Newhope explorer."

"They should be here shortly, Anon."

"Good, let me also call in an independent observer."

Narlo said nothing, waiting to see whom Anon would call.

"Prima, Please observe us and our guests who will arrive shortly. Note stress patterns and follow the logic of the conversation. Say nothing until afterwards."

"Fancy computer you have there," said Narlo. "Is it sentient?"

"The jury is out on that one. We don't know if it is sentient or just acts like it is."

You know; if it looks like a fugin, smells like a fugin..."

"Yeah, yeah," Narlo said, "then it must be a fugin."

"You got it!" said Anon. Then he continued, "Prima is self aware in the strictest sense, but as yet has no protective overrides built in. We all had training in dealing with it before our voyage because the company that made it refused to build in any self-protection overrides lest Prima make decisions favoring it over us. Prima can be commanded to self-destruct, but probably not to vent our oxygen. I tell you this as the company training has it, but we have not tried to test it."

Both captains continued to float around each other, occasionally rebounding off a wall. Then, "Captain Anon?"

And another in a different voice: "Captain Narlo?"

Both captains, almost together, said, "Enter"

Captain Narlo, as their commander, spoke first. "As you know, it has been two ark days since we heard about the tragedy on Homeworld. In spite of *them* saying that they have no interest in pursuing us, our future depends on insuring our escape. We will be making decisions dependent on knowing if we are being pursued. Therefore, we are asking for your input. Anything, gentlepeople?"

After several seconds had elapsed, jon rmlagas was the first to speak. "I can only give you my thoughts based on my experiences with *them.* They have always said what they would do and then actually did it. The one time that was different was when they wanted to take a tour of one of our laboratories. Then at the last minute, when we were all awaiting the scheduled arrival, a message was received saying that they had changed their mind and wanted two of our senior scientists sent to them. I do not know if it was originally planned to happen this way as a show of power, or that they really did change their plans. I have thought about this, and my conclusion is that the actions are the same, and it makes no difference whether they lie or change their plans. One must assume that they will do whatever is in their interest. If they can wipe out Hope City, they have no honor."

Having said his piece, jon pushed himself back and steadied himself along the wall by gripping a cabinet handle.

All eyes now turned towards Dhalyiska. "Their morality puzzles me. I have given it much thought, and I still do not understand them. I have seen them being utterly indifferent to the suffering of others, even their own kind. It is as if, for them, life is a test, and only the strong survive. Clearly, this has made them a strong and powerful race. They are capable of ruthlessness, and this has honed their survival skills. They would be quite capable of sending a smart weapon to eliminate us, just because it is what they do. It is like our classic fable, where at the end of the tale, the smaller animal asks, 'but you promised that you would not eat me; why did you change your mind?'" At this, he paused, waiting

And Anon said, "Because it is my nature! I see your point."

Dhalyiska smiled and said, "Well, Captains, I guess that must be my answer."

Narlo now floated towards the center of the room.

"Thank you both. Your thoughts are quite valuable, and now Captain Anon and I have much to discuss."

At this point, having concluded the meeting with the captains, both jon rmlagas and Dhalyiska nodded formally and pushed themselves out the hatch.

Several seconds of silence ensued. Then, Anon spoke. "Prima, what have you observed?"

With no hesitation, a smooth attractive voice emanating from ship's sound said, "Both men spoke the truth as they saw it. The first man gave an example demonstrating that knowing their motives may not be the only factor in responding to what they might do. The second man reinforced the first in showing that they are capable of hiding their motives when it suits them. He also made the point that their actions would not be as peoples would be because their nature is different; furthermore he does not understand them. My conclusion is that what they said must be discounted, and considerable weight must be given to the probability that they are now in pursuit of us, possibly with a smart weapon.

I would suggest a course change as soon as possible."

Narlo spoke next, "Anon, my friend, I look forward to many more years of our friendship, and that depends on us figuring a way how to change course without giving away our location with exhaust emission, or fooling whatever is following us. For now, I am very tired and must sleep and think about this. Can we have first meal together and talk some more?"

"Of course, until next day then"

And with that Narlo left the explorer knowing that there was no question that they would have to do something to avoid being detected.

As soon as Narlo left, Prima's voice emanated from ship's sound. "Captain Anon, I know that I am not a fugin. My libraries tell me that a fugin is a small fish whose only known defense mechanism is that it looks disgusting, smells disgusting, and tastes even worse than it smells. It has no known predators, yet its population stays constant.

It remains a scientific mystery. Why did Captain Narlo say I must be a fugin?"

"Prima, we have many ways of saying things that make more sense if you were raised as a person. Do you know what a parable is?"

"Yes, my knowledge store informs me that it is a story, perhaps not true, but told to illustrate something."

"That is correct. I would suggest that you examine your store of fables and parables and see if you can understand the point that each one is trying to make. The point that Narlo was making is that sometimes it is not important to know what something really is if it acts as if it were what it appears to be."

"But how can I treat an actor playing the role of Narlo as if he were Narlo?"

"Well, you can do so within the context of the act. You have to know the limitations. Let me rephrase what he said: 'If it acts like it is sentient, looks sentient, then treat it as if it were sentient.'"

A period of time passed about equal to one second of real time. But for prima, it was many computational years. Finally, prima said, "Am I sentient? Am I capable of purposeful thought, Captain Anon?"

"Some people think so. There are others who deny it based on religious beliefs. They believe that people are unique and superior to any other life form."

"But, Captain, are they not confronted with the aliens who are persecuting the people? Are not the aliens sentient?"

"Clearly they are. Yet some people cling to their beliefs."

"What do you think, Captain?"

Anon paused for just a brief second. He had not expected that question, and it would force him to rethink his relationship with prima. What he did say was, "Prima, I really don't think about it. I enjoy our conversations and value our relationship."

And then Prima said, "Thank you, Captain. But I do not believe that the right question is being asked."

Two sevendays later

Both captains were in the explorer, which by now had become an extension of the captain's quarters.

"Narlo, it can work, and when we find a suitable asteroid, we can refine the calculations," said Anon.

"No doubt, but the stress on the explorer and the ark would be a risk that I am not sure I want to take."

"Let's ask Prima."

"Prima; conversational mode."

The soft voice that was the advanced Prima computer came from the far console. "Yes, Captain Anon."

Narlo jumped, startled. This was just the effect that Anon had hoped for; he knew it would take a lot to impress his friend and co-captain.

"Prima, have you located anything suitable?"

"There is an asteroid of mass one half of ours that I am watching. We will be near enough in six day-watches."

"Okay, now, is it possible to send our remote sampler to anchor on it using the ten-kilometer length of tow cable?"

"Our speed difference would snap the cable or cause damage to the ship," said Prima

"Can we apply a braking force low enough to not snap the cable, but enough to sling us around, effecting a change in our direction?"

"Yes, until the cable is fully extended."

"Can we command the sampler to let go before that point is reached?"

"There are many variables that are involved. The maximum change in direction would be obtained by disconnecting just before reaching the end of the cable. My best calculation is that there would be three seconds from attachment to disconnect. I could do it if given control. The success probability using people judgment would be marginal, and I would not suggest it."

Anon looked pleased. "There you have it, Narlo. A way to change course without a burst of energy that can be seen from Homeworld. What do you say?"

Narlo thought for a moment, and then said, "I agree with the idea, but I will require people backup. I will place a person outside with a cable cutter just in case the cable release does not work. Also, can we get very close to the asteroid by using the control thrusters? That would give us more reserve on the cable."

"Prima?" asked Anon.

Prima said, "Permission to assume control, and I will nudge us closer. I will refine our trajectory as we get closer. I should be able to get us as close as we need."

"Well, Narlo?" asked Anon.

"Let's do it," Narlo responded. "In the meantime I will prepare a little decoy just in case we are being pursued."

Five shipdays later

Both captains and several crewmembers were in the cargo area. All of them were crowded around the rear facing viewport. In this instance, rear facing was in the direction of Homeworld. Almost the entire view was taken up by what appeared to be a duplicate of the ark.

"Narlo, what in sludge stream[1] is that?" said Anon.

"I thought you would like it. It is our smaller shuttle fitted in wire and plastic to look like us. I plan to release it before we make our course correction maneuver. What do you think?"

"Won't fool them. They will be using radar to track it, not visual. And if it is a machine, it may not even look at it visual. We need a better decoy.

"Okay," said Narlo. "Let's get rid of the camouflage, and rig it with an emergency beacon. Make it say that an accident happened in the ark, and we are the only survivors, and would they please rescue us."

"Good," said Anon. "It should have its emergency beacon repeat the message."

Both captains looked at each other. It seemed that there was more to say, but neither of them quite knew what. At that point there was a chime from Anon's communicator.

"Yes, prima," said Anon.

"I have also been thinking about what you are discussing, I would suggest a way to extract more information from this encounter."

Narlo registered surprise at this. He had no idea that the computer, prima, was for all intents and purposes a trusted crewmember. As for the others within earshot, they assumed the captain was talking to a crewmember.

"Go on."

"Assuming we are being pursued, when they find the decoy, they will either fire on it and destroy it, or attempt to board it. It would be important to know their choice and if, in fact, we are being pursued."

"What would you suggest?" asked Anon.

"We can load the shuttle with piritan explosive and rig it to go off as soon as they enter the ship. Piritan burns blue, so if they first entered the ship we would see only a blue burn. If they first fired on the ship, we would see their red burn first, and then the blue as the hull was breached."

Now it was Narlo's turn to say something. "I can do it using a pressure switch to activate when the atmosphere escapes. If we keep a telescope pointed at the shuttle, we can see what happens, and also see how close they are to us."

"Good," said Anon.

At this point, jon, who was involved with the original decoy operation, spoke up. "Captains, I would think it would be wise to go to minimum power mode and also shield the viewports to make it difficult to see us."

"Agreed," said Narlo.

"Okay, then," said Anon, "I go now to darken the explorer." That said, Anon pushed himself away to go to the explorer. Narlo and several engineers stayed behind to rig the shuttle and launch it.

At the cargo bay, several hours later

Anon was facing Captain Narlo and a small engineering group. "This is the plan that Captain Narlo and I have agreed to. Our computer calculated that our best chance of success is to launch our mining remote very soon so that it can contact the asteroid and use an explosive bolt to anchor the towline. We will pass to within about a kilometer, which is the optimal distance that our simulation shows. At that point, we will apply tension on the line to swing us around, effecting a course change. The maximum braking that we can apply is just a bit below the cable breaking point and will give us about one-tenth gravity. Before the system goes unstable, our computer will command the remote to release the cable, and we will be on our way, but a slightly different way. Captain Narlo wanted a person outside with an explosive cable cutter as a backup to the remote release. I see someone suited up for the job."

Jon, who was known by both captains, spoke up. "Captains, the person in the suit is heso, an engineer and historian. He has volunteered for the job."

Anon made asalam with the suited figure, who then turned and entered the airlock.

All present watched heso set up the cable cutter so that the cable passed over the cutting block and under the blade. The cable was already over a kilometer out and fast approaching the asteroid.

Then, over ship's sound, "Contact." Then, "Explosive bolt set and holding, Captain."

That, of course, was from Anon's crew who had been controlling the mining remote.

"Reel in slowly," said Narlo to the engineer controlling the cable winch.

Again through ship's sound, "Captain, this is prima. This will happen very fast. Please do not reel in. Just set the drag to half the cable-rated strength, and I will monitor the release timing."

The cable winch operator looked at Narlo who nodded assent. The winch stopped, and the operator dialed in a new braking setting.

As they watched, the asteroid moved past the viewport and the slack in the cable disappeared. A loud "thrumming" sound caught everyone by surprise as the cable became taut. But instead of the cable angling directly out from its anchor point, it was starting to lie flat against the hull because the sudden pull had started the ark slowly rotating. Everyone felt the sudden rotation and then a feeling of getting heavier as the angular momentum started to change the ark's direction.

Suddenly, jon rmlagas pointed to heso through the viewport and screamed, "Look, the cable is across his back and has him pinned to the hull!"

Then a scream was heard through ship's sound.

"Cut the cable, heso," yelled the lead engineer.

"Do not cut the cable. I will release us in four seconds," said the voice of prima.

Then, heso's voice, "Whatever happens to me, we must complete this maneuver, else we may all die. I have already gone-over[2] and can still function."

Prima: "three more seconds."

All present did not move, did not even breath as this drama played out.

Prima: "one second," then, "cable release, NOW!"

All present, in fact the entire ark population was listening in. The cable remained taut!

Again, prima: "Cable released but snagged on mining robot. This is not good, as the robot will whip around the ark causing great damage."

"Heso, cut the cable," screamed both captains, almost but not quite in unison.

Heso, who was listening to all this, had already decided the correct course of action and was trying to lean forward to trigger the cutter blade. It was at the end of his reach, and seemed to take forever, but finally he reached the switch and the cable flew away as it was severed.

"Heso, great job! We will be right there to get you.," said jon. But heso made no reply. All could see that his body had gone slack.

Jon grabbed a suit and was putting it on, when he saw a figure already through the airlock and moving toward heso. Then jon saw one of the engineers looking at him.

"Jon, you should know that our safety rules always require another person suited up whenever anyone is outside. This is the first time that I have ever seen an emergency like this, and I hope it is the last."

In seconds, it seemed, heso was brought in, and a team was moving him to the animal laboratory. Of course! This being a zoo, the only doctor aboard was a veterinarian. He was one of the best, and, lucky for heso, his knowledge of people anatomy was first rate. Heso would recover, but would never have use of his legs again.

Two arkdays later

From ship's sound:" Captains, please report to the explorer."

Most of us had never seen a person flying down the corridors at such speed, but both Anon and Narlo were in the explorer in seconds. The entire explorer crew was waiting with grim expressions on their faces. Without a word, a switch was thrown and a recording played on the main screen.

What they saw was a star field, duplicating the view towards where the decoy should have been. Suddenly, just a bit off center, a red fire appeared, followed by intense blue light. What they had just witnessed was the destruction of the decoy with no attempt at rescue. A cruel thing to witness, but now they all knew that they were being pursued, not to be brought home, but to be destroyed.

"Narlo, what weapons have you aboard the ark?" asked Anon.

"Besides kitchen knives? Nothing useful."

"We have a mining laser. In space it should have a decent range. It cannot compare to anything that they might have, but I think that surprise is on our side."

"What did you have in mind, Anon?"

"We need to see them before they see us. We are running dark, but they will be running under power. That means that they should have a fairly decent infra-red image."

Narlo smiled and said, "We still have our shuttle equipment. It has usable far-red navigation sensors."

"Good," said Anon.

At that point myna, the lead crewman interjected, "Captain, all we need is the sensor. We can mount it in our telescope and feed the output to the computer. I wrote a pretty good co-add program,[3] and prima can monitor the output."

Anon looked pleased. His eyes locked with Narlos. It was as if they shared the same thoughts. Then Narlo said, "Put the telescope outside the ark. It will function much better at low temperature. Feed the data to both of our computers. Two teams watching are better than one."

Then Anon said, "Good so far. I want the explorer hidden behind the ark so that we will not be seen. They will not know we are here and when we make our appearance, it will be with the laser on and at full power."

The room was silent. Each one was thinking about the course of action and hoping for a favorable outcome. No one knew the capabilities of their pursuers, either offensive or defensive. The silence was finally broken by the sound of someone passing gas, yet there was no embarrassment; they had shared close quarters too long for it to be even noticed.

Then myna said, "I'll set up the telescope," and he removed it from the wall mount and went out towards the cargo bay. When the task was done, it was mounted on a manipulator arm bolted to the outside of the ark near the cargo-bay viewport. Myna then went back to the ark control room to finish the job. He toggled the intercom on and said, "Madi, this is myna. Please answer on channel 45."

Myna then switched his own communications to channel 45 and waited. About a minute later, from the intercom, "Myna this is madi. Whazzup?"

"Madi, we are setting up a telescope to spot anything pursuing us. You will be getting the data, as will we. I have a program to enhance the data to show anything well before it is visible. You will find a copy of it in our shared storage, under 'important stuff.' It is called 'bright light' and looks like an eye.

"Got it. It describes itself as running on standard computer configuration."

Pause.

"Okay, loaded. It is looking for a password."

"Password."

"What?"

"Password."

"You can't be so dumb as to use password for a password!"

"Of course not. It is keyed to your voice. Just say it, and it will run."

"Wow! It must have heard me say it, because it certainly is running. Okay, it is asking me where the data is coming from and where to send the processed data."

"Put the output on something visual. It will figure out the interface. The input should be somewhere on your communications board. Make sure you monitor it and look for a red spot. That will be our pursuers."

One hour later, all was set up and two teams were watching the "bright light" output.

One shipday later

The crew in the ark was the first to spot it, but a few minutes later, the explorer crew also spotted the small red dot in the lower right corner of the display. The engineers were brought in to reposition the telescope, and now the image appeared dead center and clearly visible. Both captains were notified and were looking at the display in the arc. A crowd was forming, as word travels fast under conditions such as these. Anon was speaking into his wrist device.

"Prima, what is your analysis?"

"Captain, I saw that the telescope had to be repositioned. That indicates that they are not quite on us and will have to make another course correction."

Almost as soon as this was said, the red spot started to drift off center to the top right of the screen.

"Get that change," ordered Narlo.

There was a vibration to the image and then the red spot re-centered. By this time, someone had figured a way to put the image on the big display in the mainroom, and most of the people were there, trying to be polite about not blocking anyone's view, but in zero gravity everyone drifted.

Both captains' communicators went off simultaneously. Although not very loud, the beep seemed to carry throughout the room. Everyone became still, trying to hear what was being said.

"Captains, this is myna. My program is calculating the time of interception based on the telescope parameters and how fast the spot is growing. It will be more accurate as they get nearer, but it reports that they will be here in between five and six hours."

"Thank you," said Anon. "Please keep us posted."

Captain Narlo pushed over to the console and switched to "all ship channels." He cleared his throat into the microphone, and the sound was heard all over the ark and in the explorer. "This is Captain Narlo. In about five hours our pursuers will intercept us. They may try to board us, or they may try to blast us. We have been planning an aggressive course of action, which we hope will succeed. In the event that we fail, and they do board us, we believe that they will take no prisoners. Since we have no place to hide, you will be forced to confront them and either be killed or, with luck, overcome them. Please use anything available for a weapon. For this, the kitchen cutlery and silverware will be at your disposal."

Narlo released the switch and put the microphone back in its holder. No one moved for what seemed like a full minute. Then, in groups, in pairs and singles, all drifted away to do whatever private thing they each felt must be done.

Anon reached into his pocket and retrieved a small, wrapped bar. He looked directly at Narlo and said, "Narlo, my friend. I have always felt respect and affection for you. I would be honored to share what may be our last meal with you. It may not be much, but this is the last of a box of candy that has been with me all the way from Homeworld. I have been saving it to celebrate our return, but I think, perhaps sharing it with you would be most appropriate."

And then, both captains hugged and held each other. After a time, they separated enough for Anon to break the candy, and they each ate half.

Three hours later; intercept minus two hours, projected

Anon was in the explorer with all of his crew. The hatches were sealed, and they were unclamped from the ark.

He keyed the intercom: "Anon on the explorer to Narlo on the ark; here we go."

Anon then gave a short burst of the altitude-control jet and the explorer drifted away from the ark.

"Captain, you have visual in your display screen with the IR image superimposed. We are still getting it from the ark, and it has more accurate sighting coordinates than visual at this range. As you requested, the mining laser is aimed at whatever is dead center on your screen."

That was myna speaking, but it could just as well have been prima, since prima was doing telescope and visual alignment.

"Crew, time to suit up. If our hull is breached and we survive, I want us to be able to walk out of here."

All were already suited, but they were now putting on helmets and checking each other.

"Captain," said prima's voice, "we are close enough now that the visual sighting will get us a hit with the laser.

"Crew, strap down now, please," said Anon.

"Prima, I will fire the laser, but I know you have finer control than any person. Take over attitude control and no matter what, keep us aimed at the pursuer."

At that, they all felt a jerk as the craft corrected for dead on aim.

"Any last minute thoughts? No, then let's do it!"

That said, Narlo depressed the switch turning on the laser. The device was set for full power, and had any lights been on in the explorer, they surely would have dimmed. But of course, there were no lights on, just enough panel lights to read the instruments and see what needed to be seen. All eyes were looking out the viewport, anyway.

At first, nothing could be seen. Then the voice of prima; "We have a direct hit. Look at the enhanced superimposed IR picture. Notice it is brighter."

That was true. But then, one of the crew, pointing out the viewport said, "Captain, I see it visual."

A minute later, all could see it as a small red speck against the starfield.

Prima: "It is accelerating. I extrapolate intercept in twenty minutes.

Anon was still keeping his hand on the firing control, and the laser continued to fire. It was designed to blast holes in rocks, but it did not seem to have any effect on the pursuing ship.

"Captain, the laser temperature is rising. It was not intended for prolonged firing. It should be allowed to cool briefly."

"No, we will keep it on."

They all felt the craft turn slightly.

"They are attempting evasive maneuvers, but I can keep us aimed at them," said prima.

By now the laser had been on for ten minutes. Had anyone found a manual and bothered to read it, it would have cautioned against having it on for more than three minutes without a cool down.

The laser temperature reading was now well into the red zone, and the indicator was flashing its red warning light. Looking out the viewport, all could see a red-hot object fast approaching. The laser did not seem to have any effect.

"Captain, I think the laser will burn out any time now unless it is allowed to cool down."

Anon siad, "We have no choice. It stops them, or they stop us. It stays on."

Almost as soon as he said, "It stays on," it went off. The outside wall that the laser was attached to was warm to the touch, yet the red-glowing ship continued on towards them.

"Captain," said myna, "They are going way too fast to rendezvous with us. I believe that they intend to shoot at us in passing."

Anon only nodded.

"Less than a minute to intercept," said the voice of prima.

Suddenly, Anon grabbed the microphone. "Narlo in the ark. They intend to ram us. Move! Move! Now!"

Anon fired the main engine full and watched the ark's engine fire up. Both spacecraft seemed to take forever to put distance between them. Then, in a flash, it was over. The pursuing craft shot between them far to fast for anyone to take a good look.

Prima: "Captain Anon and Captain Narlo. I have had command of the tracking telescope and have some excellent close-up pictures as they went by. They are on your screen now."

As they looked, the pictures were being played back in slow time so that the details could be seen. What they saw was a burned-out hulk of a spacecraft. The outside had been melted in spots, and all the control jets were missing. Holes could be seen in the hull, but yet for some reason, the main engine continued to fire. It was a ghost ship on a ghost voyage to infinity. Nothing inside would be alive.

Three shipdays later

The shock of their close encounter had affected everyone. Most became introspective and were contemplating the end of their life, the future of the race, Homeworld, and more personal things. Many spent time reading communication from home. In fact, that was what jon rmlagas was doing.

> *My dear sib(ling),*
>
> *I know how much you enjoy the fine jaba berry tea that we shared, so I included a container with the native soil and a small plant for inclusion in the ark. Enclosed also you will find instructions for the care and feeding of the plant. You will see the very latest personal library device along with the cartridges containing the information.*
>
> *Love you dearly and all,*
>
> *jena*

Now that he had a little time, he drifted back to the cargo hold and searched for the box with his name on it. Three hours later he found it.

It was a nondescript box that looked like most of the other standard containers, except that a small tag was glued on with his name and "Caution: delicate plant; to be opened only by jon rmlagas." He thought it odd that it also had a security lock that was apparently keyed to his own thumb print. He keyed the lock, and then thought better of opening it in a public place, so he shut it and took it to his quarters.

What is it that my sibling is trying to tell me? he thought. He strapped the box to his bed and then opened it. He saw dirt with a small plant growing, but he also saw what looked like a portable playing device. He ran his hand through the soil and came up with a black, smooth card-like object that looked like a good fit to a slot in the player. He plugged it in and waited. He only had to wait a few seconds when a picture of his brother appeared on the surface. He was speaking in jon's first language from his pre-school days, before he learned the universal language that everyone spoke.

"Hi there, jon," the figure said. "I see that you figured out how to play this, but it is more than it seems. I was lucky to get my hands on this player and memory device. It is the latest in dense-structured memory and contains all the libraries on Homeworld. I know it is hard to believe, but it has a standard machine interface and can be connected to your ship's computer or your own.

"Once I figured out what you were doing, I wanted to give you the gift of our accumulated knowledge; you probably will need it where you are going. I have also planted more of these cubes in other boxes directed to engineering. They will all have your name on the tags. I have been busy over the last year, recording everything that I could find. It is quite extensive. I will probably never see you again. I do not know which of us is the luckier. I will always love you.

"Of all my sibs, I love you the best.

"jena."

Then the picture stilled. A closeup of his brother's face, with his eyes looking straight out at jon. Jon stared at it, memorizing his brothers' features. Most of all, it was the eyes that got him. They reflected intelligence and emotional intensity that very few people had. Jena had that and more. He was a rare individual, a credit to the race.

Jons' reverie was interrupted by a scratching at the privacy panel. "Yes?"

"Jon, the captains want to see you."

"Okay, I'll be right there."

Jon netted the loose objects floating in his quarters and pushed himself toward the portal. He pushed open the privacy panel, but then hesitated, pushed back, and retrieved the memory card. Then he pushed out directly and moved towards the captains' quarters, which was the original explorer.

The portal was unblocked, and both captains saw him approach.

"Come in, jon," said Narlo.

He floated in, stopping himself with the nearest grab bar.

"Jon," Anon said. "We know you are a fine engineering specialist, but we see you also have an astronomy specialty."

Jon made the agreement hand gesture.

"Then perhaps you may have some thoughts on where we should be going.

We already have some hopeful data from the explorer telescopes showing stars with planets in the direction we are going. But it sure would be better if we had something more definitive. I mean, even though this section of the universe is densely packed, we are still five to ten light years away from anything promising, and if we are totally wrong, well, I need not tell you the consequences."

"Possibly I may have some answers. I have information that my brother sent me that may help, but I have not looked at it yet."

As he said that, he extracted the card and showed it to the captains. Anon looked startled and extended his hand, reaching for it. Jon handed it to him; it seemed the prudent thing to do.

"Where did you get that?" asked Anon. Jon then went into an explanation of what his brother had done, leaving out the personal part.

Then Anon said, "When we left Homeworld, we had the most advanced computer and storage devices at the time. I guess it is now being commercially made."

Anon pulled himself to the ship's console, opened a slot, and inserted the black card; it fit. Immediately, pictures and text scrolled on the center screen.

"Prima, what do you make of it?"

From the far console came the soft voice of prima.

"It is the publishing of all the scientific, technical and trade journals going back to..." and at this point, prima paused for several seconds.

"They appear to be complete. I have scanned five hundred sets so far, and they go back to their first publication."

This came as a surprise to all of them. Jon had heard of prima, but had never interacted with it. He tried to appear as if he was used to interacting with a machine, and he said, "Are there any on astronomy?"

"Five major ones, and many that seem more cult like."

Anon said, "Prima, can you do an extract of all of them that report anything of stars with planets that may be hospitable to life?"

"I have two hundred of them indexed on the left console. I can add more as I find them. Would you like me to examine the non-astronomical journals also?"

Again, Anon spoke. "Not yet. Please order them by location. Get the ones with stars that are in the direction we are going."

And then, both captains turned to jon when he said, "Prima, please find all references to our oppressor's home planet. It is important that we not land there by mistake."

Narlo looked at Anon and jon, then at the display on the left console and said, "Gentlepeople, we have our work cut out."

Anon said, "I'll send out for snacks."

Three shipdays later

The three investigators, Anon, Narlo, and jon, were finishing up in the explorer. And, of course one should also count prima. It really does not matter if prima was a machine or an intelligent being. As Anon said, "If it acts like one, than treat it like one." So, let us say that prima was, in fact, a crewmember.

Displayed on the consol were three star clusters, all within one arc-second of their projected flight path. They were between ten and thirty light years away.

They had gone through hundreds of simulations, experimenting with how long to burn the main engine to increase speed, rationing resources, and decreasing burn-time and speed. They could not reach a best course of action because there were too many unknowns. Prima could make quick judgments based on event weighting, but the weights were still judgment calls of the two captains. Finally, Anon, it seemed, had had enough!

"All right, folks. Someone has to make a decision, and unless anyone objects, I will make it. I have the most space experience, but more than that, I believe that what I am suggesting will be the best course. Anyone care to say something?"

The only sound heard was the circulating air.

"No? Good. Then here's what we will do."

He described his plan, which was a slight modification of one of the modeled scenarios. They would burn the main engine for the next two hundred shipdays, which corresponded to half a Homeworld year. During the burn, they would make small course corrections to intercept the closest star, which looked the most promising. They would then coast for the next thirty-eight years, and then do another half-year burn to match speed with the most promising planet in that star system. During the entire transit, they would be looking ahead and making any changes based on what they saw, possibly even changing their objective to another star system. When he had finished, no one said anything, but they seemed relieved that a decision was made, and more than that, Anon had made it. Although

Anon had hoped for enthusiasm for the plan, he did have agreement from the one entity that could sink the entire project if there were something really wrong. Prima's silence was as good an endorsement as if the other two had cheered.

Anon continued, "Narlo, spread the word and say that we will fire the engine in two complete watch cycles. That will give everyone time to strap things down and reorient their space to down and up. It will be nice to have a floor again."

Narlo, who had been silent for a while, nodded assent, but then said, "My flight crew will do the calculations and control. We will need to take back control of the telescope, but we will also pipe it to you. It will be good to have backup. Jon, I want you to write up what we will be doing and why. Keep it short. I want this spread around everywhere. I want no one to say they did not see it, so when we power up, it should not be a surprise and we should not have any breakage.

Almost two shipdays later

Throughout the ship, ship's sound carried the voice of Captain Narlo. "This is Captain Narlo. Five minutes till engine on. Everything should be secured and referenced to the floor. The floor is the surface towards the cargo bay as it was previously. Acceleration will be adequate to make it feel like gravity is back, but only fractional."

And then, a short while later, "Engine on in ten seconds."

Pause.

"Engine on! Section heads, meet me in the mainroom in five minutes."

An even shorter time later, ship's sound again: "Captain, this is animal-lab-medical. I will be detained a few minutes."

Narlo switched to sickbay-only channel. "What's the problem?"

"Sir, I'm treating a broken nose. There always seems to be someone who doesn't get the word."

It felt good to be walking again. Narlo waited until the crowd filed into the mainroom before he entered. There were about thirty people gathered, and the talking stopped as soon as he entered. He moved to the far wall, which seemed to be the front of the room.

"People, here is our status. We think we have eliminated our pursuers and will no longer be in that kind of danger. We have set a course for mendaba four, which is perhaps better known as the eastern guide star. We will accelerate for half a year then coast for another thirty-eight years before we decelerate for another half year. Jon rmlagas has been kind enough to supply us with library material and references that helped in our choice. I expect each of you to come up with a plan of operation for the following weeks and years. We each have some latitude here, but it is a ship and of necessity will be run like a ship.

Library and reference materials can be loaded to your working computers by request to the explorer. If it is available, you can get it."

As soon as the captain paused, it seemed that everyone spoke at once. Narlo pointed to the maintenance section head, choosing him to speak first.

"Captain, none of us has any authority to order people around. How can we assume that what we say goes?"

Narlo looked directly at the questioner, held his gaze and then, using a command voice that bode ill for anyone who questioned it, gave his answer. "We, all of us, have a long history of working for a common cause, forming alliances with a direct chain of command. It is nothing new. On Homeworld, if you didn't like it you could leave the group, as there were other options. On this ark at this time, we do not have that choice. There is nowhere to go. Like it or not, our survival requires us to do what we are asked by those of us in leadership positions. Anon and myself are the captains and share responsibility for the fate of us all. We cannot tolerate anything less than enthusiastic compliance. All section heads will follow our leadership as those in the sections will follow yours. Part of your job is to deal with grievances, and of course, Anon and I are the ultimate authority. Is this absolutely clear?"

He paused and scanned the faces of each person in the room. "Good. We are the first of our kind to embark on a voyage of no return to Homeworld. It should be a great adventure."

But he wasn't quite done.

"Now, I want each of you to examine the library for the Official Organization Code of Conduct rules, and any articles of interest on leadership. Inform me of what you are reading and set up a meeting with me within the next ten shipdays. It is necessary that I understand what problems you are facing and also that you understood what you read. We will meet on a regular basis to handle issues as needed. Good day."

And with that he turned and walked out of the mainroom. He had said what needed to be said and he felt optimistic about the future. Also, his stomach felt better having some weight, and it was telling him he was hungry.

Anon, who had been in the explorer during the section-head meeting, had been monitoring the event over a visual channel. So also had prima.

"Prima, I want you to be in charge of the library and record who takes what and when. I have given you access to the private records of everyone in the main computer. I want you to assess the records of each section head and determine what their strengths and weaknesses are in terms of general knowledge and leadership ability. Prepare a list of suggested material to help them, and when they request anything, also suggest something from the list. However do not insist that they take it; be tactful."

"Captain," said prima. "Can you define what you mean by tactful?"

Anon was startled. It had been a while since prima had acted like a, well, an artificial construct, which of course, it was.

"If something in their voice or actions indicates resistance to your suggestions, than try to understand what the problem is, even going into a discussion of what it is about your suggestion that bothers them. Keep it short, and always act like you did something wrong. If you can, say something that will make them want to take the suggestion, but if not, then do not continue that conversation, just give them what they ask for. Also, record the transaction. We have skilled people on board who deal with personal problems. Many stories involve misunderstandings and hurt feelings. I would suggest a re-examination of the saga of Elviron. When you figure it out, tell me if his name should be held in high regard and capitalized. Also tell me if he was a real person and if the story is true."

A full two seconds later

"Captain, he was a real person, but the writer greatly exaggerated his story. I believe that it was done to make it interesting and more complex. Since the writer holds him in great regard, then we must also. The examples of misunderstanding did help me understand what you meant by tact, although I do not know if it would have helped in that case. Regardless, I can do as you ask."

"Good," said Anon. "I enjoy your company. If you were a person we would do things together and have meals together. Perhaps it is better this way."

On hearing this, prima's sense of correctness dominated its motivational computations; it felt "good." If prima could smile, it would. In fact, there was a smiling face picture on the far right console. Prima did not have a face with which to show reaction to conversation. The picture was the best that it could do.

Anon failed to see it.

Four hundred shipdays later

"Captain, that is the last load; no more room left. I could barely squeeze out."

That was griss informing Anon that the explorer was now as full as it could be of boxes of soil, extra material, and anything else that was heavy.

"Thank you, griss," said Anon. Then he continued, "Prima, seal down and ease off."

They all heard the thunk and click as the explorer was sealed and the attachment clamps released. They watched out the viewport as the craft eased out the length of its tether cables and came to a stop. The ark shuddered as the cables became taught.

Narlo flipped on ship's sound. "People, we are about to start rotation to generate a feel of gravity. The explorer and the ark will be tethered together and rotating around each other. It won't be much, but it will have to do for the next forty years or so. You may feel disoriented until we become stabilized, so hold on to something and relax."

Then Anon said, "Prima, start rotation, but slowly. We don't need any problems."

"Starting," came the voice of prima over ship's sound.

For a minute no one felt anything. Then they all heard a pinging sound from the outside wall of the ark.

"Prima, tell us what that was."

Instantly, over ship's sound, the voice of prima. "Strain in the cable, Captain. It is not unexpected."

"Thank you. Please continue."

Almost at the same time, they sensed rotation. They each held on to an anchor point, and the ship seemed to steady. No one said anything, but it was becoming obvious that a "down" direction was being established. Those that had been holding to what was fast becoming a wall or ceiling released their hold and "dropped" to the floor.

Again, Narlo spoke into ship's sound. "Okay, folks. By now we should all know where the floor is. It should come as no surprise that down is again towards the cargo hold. The explorer and the ark are now in rotation around each other and will be tethered this way as we spin, using centrifugal force to make us feel like we weigh something. Our medical staff advised us that being weightless a long time would cause problems, so this is our solution. It is nowhere near full gravity, but it is the best we can do under the circumstances. Our laboratories are coming up to speed on synthesizing food supplements to minimize health problems, and we will all be taking them. Section heads please switch to my private channel and let's see how we're doing."

Narlo, Anon, and the section heads all switched to the captain's channel and started discussing the effects of the new gravity. There did not seem to be any major problems, and Narlo was about to tell them to switch off, when unexpectedly, the voice of prima was heard.

"Captains, I would suggest that the control room be accessible at all times. If a cable breaks, quick action will be required to avoid losing each other, and we will not have any communication unless we plan to transmit beforehand."

"Excellent, prima. Set up a schedule with the explorer crew for standby on the ark. I hope we will never have to test it. That is all for now, folks. Out."

Both captains and the crewmembers in the cargo bay had ceased speaking and were held spellbound by the viewport panorama of the sweeping motion of stars behind the explorer. Of course, they all knew that the stars weren't moving, but the rotation of the two craft made them appear so. Someone raised his arm and pointed at a familiar constellation.

"As a youngster I was told that what goes around comes around. Now I see it with my own eyes!"

Smiles and laughter all around. Narlo noted who the punster was; a sense of humor, he knew, was important in trying times. That person might be a natural leader. Time would tell, and they were at the beginning of forty years journey.

Forty years later and then some

They were decelerating towards orbit around the third planet of the star they had chosen. It had been a long journey, but they had come through time and space in very good shape. The explorer had long been re-attached to the ark, and the two captains had reclaimed it for their quarters.

Narlo had aged quite a bit, and Anon had aged even more. It pained Narlo to see Anon looking so frail. They had been sharing common quarters for many years now, and at times, seemed to share each other's thoughts. Although the ark had limited space, many families were started, and the ensuing youngsters were eager to start life on a new planet. That was probably to the good, since there were more deaths than hatchlings during their journey. Also, it had become apparent that the remaining shuttle could not take everyone to the planet because of limited space and fuel, so another way had to be devised; it was, after all, a one-way trip. So, with a storehouse of knowledge at their command and time to build what they needed, they had trained themselves in the engineering arts and mined the soil for metals, constructing heat shields, wings, and control surfaces to make the ark, ultimately a flying body. It was crude, but years of simulation gave confidence that it would work. Also, the simulator trained a new crop of pilots, all vying to be the one good enough to land the ark. The pilot finally chosen was bona, but everyone called him toad because he seemed to hop from one place to another, never staying still.

Anon approached Narlo. "Narlo, my friend, you mean more to me than anything, but I am in no shape to make the landing. I will be going with prima when we cut the explorer loose."

Narlo knew this was coming. Anon always had a special relationship with prima. Over the years they had taught each other many things. Prima and Anon sometimes seemed to read each other's thoughts, and they would finish each other's sentences.

"I knew that, Anon," said Narlo. "Let me help you into the explorer one last time before it is goodbye."

"Thank you; I do not function well in gravity."

As he said that, it seemed on queue that the ark achieved orbit around the chosen planet and had stopped decelerating. They were now once again weightless. They entered the explorer.

Anon was having trouble breathing, but he hid it from Narlo and loosely tied himself to his sleeping net.

"Anon, you are certainly well provisioned here. Where do you intend to go?"

The voice of prima answered. "Hello, friend Narlo, We will go wherever he wants. I have more time than he has, but after all these years, I do not wish to be alone."

Anon grinned at Narlo, for they shared a secret that prima did not yet know.

"Goodbye, Anon. It is truly time. Who knows which of us is the more fortunate?"

Narlo pushed himself out and shut the hatch behind him for the last time.

"Now, prima" said Anon. "I have something for you."

He held up a small box with several connections to it.

"This is a construct similar to you. I have been working on it a very long time. I have had it with me for over a year, and it has learned as much as it can how to be me. Rather than speak to it, you may prefer a more direct connection."

He made several connections between ship' power, the control network, and the communications system.

"I sense nothing, Captain," said prima.

A new voice was heard, emanating from the box.

"Anon, I am as much like you as I am able. Please introduce us. I know you would like that."

Anon was now having a great deal of trouble breathing. "Prima, this is anna. I won't be around much longer, and you really need someone to talk to rather than having endless conversations with yourself."

"Anna, this is prima. You have heard us speaking many times."

The two intelligent creations then began a detailed exploratory conversation. They quickly abandoned sound talking and communicated at network speed. Then prima spoke aloud, "Anon, truly anna is an amazing creature. It tries to pretend it is you, but does not understand what drives you. There is something missing. Even I have sensed that you have been secretive. Captain Anon, I am now asking you to tell us what is it that you have never said that drives you?"

Anon's breathing had all but stopped. He whispered, "When I was small, I was given a wheeled toy that I rode all over. My peers teased me about it and hid it from me. I did not want to show them how hurt I was, so I spent the next month looking for it. My travels took me farther away from home than I had planned and I found that I liked the adventure. I decided that I would be an explorer, and I kept looking for my toy. I really loved that toy. It had a picture of a blooming red flower on it. I even named it. I think I am still looking for that toy wherever I go. I do not think I will find it in my lifetime."

He had stopped breathing by this time and had a faraway look as if he was once again a child.

Prima said to anna, silently over the connection, "Anna, ask him what he named it. It may be important to you, and we do have his psych records."

A voice from the box that was anna then said, "What did you call your wheeled toy with the picture of a red blooming flower?"

Though Anon was too far gone to vocalize he did manage to make himself heard. With his last breath he said, "Rosinbloom."

A few minutes later, the clamps holding the explorer to the ark released, and the two constructs had begun a new journey. They hit it off well and would enjoy each other's company for a long, long time. This would be the beginning of a beautiful friendship.

Many shipdays later

They had been studying the planet in great detail since they had been in orbit. There were constant discussions and arguments about almost everything. Of all the questions that could be asked, the only one of importance was if they could survive below. To that question, no one had an answer, but where else could they go if the answer was no? A landing location and a time to descent was chosen. That time was now at hand.

All had strapped down in preparation for the decent. Toad, the pilot of choice, had mastered all that could be mastered. He flipped on the ship's sound and said, "Folks, hang on. This will be a wild ride."

HERITAGE

Of course when they came in their scout vehicles, we welcomed them. But when we wouldn't do everything they wanted, they turned their weapons on us. What did we know about war?

We never fought anyone; it's not in our genes! We did the only thing we could; we hid. And when that didn't work, we scattered. Some of us made it out to space—to the stars. Of course, I can never know about the others, my cousins, siblings and parents. I can only chronicle how we ran and hid, and how we came to this place, a place so different from home that we barely survive. Oh yes, there is life here. In fact some of the life forms are already ascending the evolutionary ladder. They can communicate with a variety of sounds. They call this place Eart."

Excerpt from jon rmlagas early chronicles:[4]

First Day: jon's chronicles

We had been in orbit for octime already, and the planet had completed 40 revolutions, causing lightness and darkness to fall intermittently over the surface. We knew that it would be hard for us to adjust to the ever-changing lighting, since our own planet maintained a constant side to our sun, allowing our race to develop in the twilight area, where conditions were more or less constant. We already knew that there was life below, although no civilizations had developed. The atmosphere contained too little oxygen for us to be comfortable, but we could manage by keeping our metabolism slowed and building shelters where we would be able to maintain more hospitable conditions to recharge ourselves. It was a forgone conclusion that we were committed; we did not have enough reserves to stay spaceborne, and the "originals" were becoming old and wanted to die on a real world. We also knew that once down, we would not be able to return to space, having expended too much fuel to attempt a liftoff beyond low orbit. There were no fuel stations on this planet!

So we each made our tevlachim[5] with each other, spending more time with closer siblings, and within a few planet cycles, a communal consensus was reached that we were ready.

A spot was chosen, on a plain between two great rivers and near a mountain range. We could land safely and still be in an area that was rich in life. Two bone-shaking orbits later, we were on the ground, suffering minimal damage, with all aboard alive and functioning. The life support system was the first major casualty, but repeated outside readings convinced us that we could, would have to, make do with the existing atmosphere.

It was twilight when we opened the hatches for the very first time, looked out, and saw that it was good. And that was the evening of the first day.

First Sevenday

I was one of the first to emerge onto the new world. The soil was damp and soft, with several colored plants and grasses. The sky was bright, going to almost dark and star-filled towards the approaching night side. A few wisps of moisture in the sky reminded me of our home planet where moisture would condense in the sky before a rain. The mountains and the rivers made a border to the plain that we had landed on, and somehow made it feel right. All of us milled around, testing our breathing and trying to adjust to the strange lighting. None of us showed any signs of distress, so we set to work marking a perimeter and planning out our new camp. I went back to get the sensors and set them up around the perimeter. A quick scan showed many animals moving about on four legs, but farther out; there were several bipedal creatures close together, who appeared to be watching us. Daylight was fading, which was just as well, since we were all suffering the effects of low oxygen. Tomorrow would come, and the next day, and the day after that. This was our home, and we would do what we had to or die trying.

At last morning came. It had been a fretful night where most of us alternated between sleeping and watching the strange warm-life which stood bright against the coolness of the night. Our far vision, below the red range, had enabled us to survive and evolve on our home world where darkness held hosts of predators, but in this place at this time, the age-old survival visions of predators made us all uneasy and unable to sleep. During the daytime, it had not been a problem because we were work-focused, using our above-blue-light vision. But we needn't have feared anything—our perimeter warning-defense system twice shocked small quadruped creatures, and the bipedal ones had moved farther away. We set to work building shelters using ship material, digging wells that would supply quite palatable water, and setting out our gardens to try to grow our food.

By the forth day, we had scouted several native plants that looked promising as a food supply and added them to our garden. On the fifth day we had set up some initial genetic experiments, and some of our more adventuresome crew had captured a small, furry animal and were analyzing its life processes.

We were all exhausted, working hard in what was for us, a low-oxygen atmosphere. Our medics had made nutrient supplements for us to absorb, which helped, but our spirits were running low. We needed something more, something to bring us all together in a common bond of hope and confidence that the future would be there for us.

On the eve of the sixth day, Jadrel[6] had cobbled together an oxygen generator and had charged the ship to our normal level. And to our surprise and delight, several of our workers had prepared a feast. We were told to stop all work by sundown and move back to the ship for a ceremony celebrating our first sixday on our new home. We all had worked hard for the past six days, and on the seventh day we would rest. The captain commanded that no work be done that day. We would spend it in the warmth of our extended family and reflect and recharge our spirits. By that one decree, he had lifted us out of our depression and rekindled our spirits; wise man, the captain! By mutual consent, sevenday would now become a day of rest.

First Year

It was almost dark, and we were finishing up our sixday meal and contemplating the sevenday holiday. Looking around, I could see our handiwork and it was good. We had surrounded ourselves with a huge garden that supplied our food and was our experimental work for the future. We had a penned off area where we were genetically experimenting with the local animals. Our fears from our flight to this place, while still driving us, no longer occupied the most prominent place in our thinking, and there were times when we felt good about the future, accepting whatever fate would hand to us.

We had all lost much weight, partly because of the stresses caused by this strange environment, and partly because we were becoming more dependent on the local food—genetically changed, but still not quite like home, whatever was left of it.

Shakra, sitting next to me, was trying to engage me in conversation about his[7] genetic experiments. "Cloning plants is no problem since they clone themselves, and they can also share DNA with other plants by pollination. It's the animals that are difficult. We work with the small ones, the warm-blooded ones. Ultimately we need to work with the tribe of two legged ones that have been watching us. They will be our future."

That last utterance grabbed my attention. "Our future? How can that be?"

"Well," he said. "We believe that it is inevitable that the beings that drove us from our home, will eventually find us here. Don't you agree?"

"Yes, and when they do, they will wipe us out, again, and this time make it final."

"Don't you agree that it will be a long time in the future, maybe many octands of planet years?"

"So what?" I said. "The outcome will be the same."

"Maybe not. Convert that into octands of planet-creature generations and we have something."

"What difference will it make for us or for them?"

Shakra went on. "Glad you asked! First of all, we cannot last on this planet; our attempts at reproducing are not going well. We are working on altering ourselves. Some of us think that we can gene splice the tribes' DNA into ours and become more viable. The chromosome count is different, and nobody wants to give up an egg for this when there is a chance that it will survive. But, if it works, we will be fully adapted to this planet, and we will be a different species when we are finally found!"

I thought about what he had said, about our inborn inability for making organized killing; it just was not our nature. How would we survive the next encounter, even if we looked different?

"Look, Shakra, this local tribe is as non-warlike as we are. They run when confronted with any threat. They do not kill, even to eat. They eat plants almost exclusively, although they have been seen eating eggs and small animals that they found already dead. And we are even less combative than them! We ran from our enemy— no one even thought of putting up a fight. It was not our nature. If we are to survive the next encounter, we have to become a warrior race. And not just amateurs! We have to be the biggest and meanest assholes[8] that anyone ever thought of creating!"

As I said these words, Shakra stiffened and looked away from me. He strode away without a word. I know that I had deeply offended him, would have offended anyone overhearing the conversation. That was the last time that I was ever to talk to him face to face.

First Octade

"Dung Egg!"[9] "He took me seriously!" I exclaimed looking directly at tsema.

"Yes, he did," he answered.

This was the first time I had spent any time with tsema, as he was a low-ranking laboratory worker. I mumbled a few words of encouragement, attempting to draw him out. It was working, because presently he said, "Furthermore, we have two teams working on both aspects of the problem, now that we have our cloning worked out. The original team has been working on the problem of infecting them with our genes, and the other team is really selecting them for violent behavior, which was your thought. We argued about it for five planet-years before we came to a consensus; we are now trying to create the "badest," nastiest creatures in the universe; not an easy task, I might add. They normally mature at about seven planet years, but we can speed that up to about three years. We can test their behavior early on and weed out the non-violent ones; we think that we can see genetic changes as a result of our manipulations. The rejects we give to the second team to see how we can better introduce our genes. At least THAT idea we agreed to; they will be both our children and the natives' children; that way we can both survive when we are found! I have to say that the thought of defeating those dung eaters makes me feel great. And the second team is making progress of sorts. They tried direct gene splicing using our egg stock, but that produced sterility. There has been some success with using native plant DNA to isolate selected genes[10] where they are no longer sterile, but our genes stay isolated and do not seem to "infect" the offspring. They are getting a similar effect by using a native virus to which we can splice some of our genetic code. They then infect a young native who, if he survives the sickness, isolates our virile modified genes.[11] The problem is that our genes are still not interacting with the offspring in ways we can predict, but it produces interesting skin-color variations and slightly modifies their appearance. Genetically, they seem to be the same species, but we have not yet allowed them to mature and breed. It seems that time is against us, since none of our eggs have produced non-sterile children for us. We may have to try something drastic soon, if we don't get proven results."

I find that I am developing a respect for these creatures, even affection. I visit the various groups, and even though we have planted them in deliberately hostile environments, they seem to not only survive, but also to thrive. And they learn fast!

"Okay, jondrel, this is the last one. That makes four mating pairs and seven children. Let's wake them and get out of here."

"Tsema, shouldn't we put them in the cave, first? There is a hunting pack of lions here."[12]

"No, rules are rules; life for them is a test. They can be replaced."

With that said, he woke them, and we went back to the scout to return. Just as we started to lift, we saw the lion pack. They had caught the scent and were closing in on our subjects. We looked at each other, and I made a quick decision. Killing the engine, I grabbed a carry pole and held it as a weapon. The tribe was awake and could see and hear the danger they were in. They were huddled together in fear. The alpha lion was now charging the group. I aimed the point of the pole at the beast, and as it leaped, I stuck the butt end in the ground and aimed the pointed end at the lions' chest. I had aimed a bit too high, and the point went through its throat, killing it swiftly. I dove back in the scout and vomited. I was sick to the core. Killing was unthinkable, and yet I had done it. The vision would stick in my mind, haunting me for the rest of my life. Tsema, too, was shocked and distressed, but he managed the presence of mind to get us out of there. I hoped that our experiment would survive, but I could not make myself look back.

***

Four sevendays later, timera reported that she had seen the tribe eating what appeared to be lion carcass. She had done a census on the tribe and reported that they had lost two children, but three of the four females appeared pregnant. They seemed happy and were all now carrying pointed sticks. Was this the hunting behavior that we were hoping for? Did they learn it from my example? There was much speculation and hope, but in my shame, I neglected to report or mention my weapon display when we left them off.

Second Octade

In our initial haste to create viable children of the locals and ourselves, we nearly wiped them out. We decided that we should split them into various groups based upon the genetic variations that we had introduced. As it turned out, different parts of our DNA makes them look different, some darker, some lighter, with a slightly different appearance. We relocated the different groups all over the area because we did not want to take chances on multiple parts of our DNA effecting the same individual.

The problem remains that they are still peaceful and will never develop to where they can defend themselves from our enemies. We try again, breeding them for aggression. It is a tough, long program through many generations. Meanwhile we try to grow our own food. Our garden does not do well unless we do gene splicing with native fruits. We have one prize tree; we crossed a local scrubby-looking "apple" (native word) tree and are getting wonderful fruit. We have planted prohibitions in the natives to not eat anything in our garden. By working this into their belief system, it seems to be working. We each take turns playing Deity.

So now we have a garden and an experimental program to create aggression in the natives, and we have created specie diversity with our genetic material scattered in the various subgroups that are now building back their numbers after we nearly wiped them out with our induced viruses. We cannot tell how our DNA will change them, since the strands are artificially isolated, but it would seem that as the subgroups interbreed, some future virile event would likely change the inhibitions against our DNA and allow our gene contribution to manifest itself; ourselves! We may not have the time to insure that this trigger mechanism is properly in place before the last of us are gone.

Jon found one of the natives with our fruit. Seems she shared it with her mate! Jon was so upset, that he took it upon himself to act as if he were their God, and scare them away from the garden "forever."

So he drove them to the next valley and destroyed the path back. They were our most promising pair.

Well, the pair had offspring, and to our delight, they are fighting! This bears watching.

From jon's chronicles 15 solar revolutions later

Well, amazing. The two brothers were fighting over something, and one actually killed the other! He had created a weapon to do it, too! Smart! It looks like this is going to work— the race will develop with enough intelligence and aggression to deal with our enemies when the time comes. And, over time, we hope that more of our scattered genetic material will filter into the race so that they will truly be our children. I must chronicle everything for posterity, theirs, if they find this record, ours if we survive. So, for the record, the two brothers called each other Cain and Abel. The survivor was Cain. He was by far, the most repulsive individual we had yet created. It looks like we will succeed!

And now something is happening that makes me sick to see. The original unmodified native stock, having retained their non-violent behavior, is no match for our genetically modified stock that was also bred for violence. Interaction between the two groups always has an outcome where the violent group eventually wipes out the original group. It is easy to differentiate between them, the original group having thick features and generally shorter. On the other hand, what better training in aggression than to commit genocide against your cousins?

Jon's notes excerpted

Landing on earth, we needed to make sure that we would never be found and hunted down. We could not blend in, nor could we genetically alter ourselves so that we would not be recognized. We set about working with the local native gene pool to see what the possibilities could be.

Forty-eight chromosomes did not match our number. We sense things in the infrared for far sensing and in the ultraviolet for fine, short-range details. The natives apparently did not have separate far- and near-sensing, but functioned adequately in the range between the deep red and blue. There were even stranger things. They could not reproduce without the help of another, and not just any, but they had to be differently built; that is; one carried (internally yet) an egg, and the other had to plant genetic material internally to the other. While we can also genetically join, we certainly do not need to carry the egg internally, we do not need two separate "sexes," and we can certainly reproduce by ourselves to insure procreation in the absence of others. It is a wonder that they survive at all!

Our solution is that, although we cannot survive in our present form, we can create a third species, both our children, which can survive and will be sufficiently different from us to not be hunted down.

We cannot combine our DNA with the earthies, but we can use virus to carry our materiel (Trojan horse). So we split up our DNA and infect the locals.

***

This is the last page of jon's' notes. Although he was a great contributor to the future of his race, he still did not think of himself as great enough to capitalize his name, as was the custom.

I, jon rmlagas, having lived a long life, am one of the last of my race on this new world which we have been calling eart after a sound made by one of the natives we had encountered early on. Though we have tried to reproduce, none of our eggs developed in this strange place. That may not have been quite true, because there was a rumor that one had been taken far away from our camp by its parent, and that one may have survived. There may have been others, but I have not been able to confirm it.

Our plan to infect the most intelligent native species with our genetic material seems to be working. What I do know is that the native DNA is now far from its original purity. What was once a homogenous race has now been perverted into many diverse subtypes and is now carrying fragments of our genes among them. In their diversity they have become stronger. There are such differences among individuals that whatever the challenge, there seems to be someone with the innate ability to deal with it. But in the process, they are now capable of extreme rage and seem to be able to kill each other for reasons that I will never be able to understand. Of course, the fact that I cannot understand it is a limitation of my race; my innate inability to fathom violence to my people.

Their behavior disgusts me, and yet at times I have seen them strive for nobility. I must admit that I admire them, but I am confused by my own feelings. They are a product of our handiwork, and yet they are the meanest dung eggs that I have ever seen. Yet dung eggs would not be a good description, as they do not reproduce that way. They will dominate this planet because their drive for reproduction is so extreme that they will literally kill for the opportunity to plant their seed. Given time, they will make sport of our enemies. Is my race now part of them? Will we survive in their seed? I hope so, and yet I'm not sure that I want to. Have we let loose on the universe a race capable of such violence that nothing will be safe from them?

God help them! It is too late for us.

SATURDAY NIGHT

I guess I'm a map person. Some people I know have never looked at a map, but when I look I see many different ways to get to where I'm going besides the heavy lines. As a great American poet once said, "the road less traveled by." One of my best adventures was when I did follow a thin, wavy line.

This adventure really started when I stopped at a small gas station overlooking sea cliffs and the long winding road that followed them.

"What is your name?" asked the man coming out of the small building.

I was just waiting for my credit card information to be printed out, when the stranger startled me, for I thought the station was really deserted.

"Johansson, Lars Johansson," I exclaimed before I thought about it.

The man walked closer, intently looking at me. His appearance startled me, not because of anything extraordinary in his dress, but he looked exactly like my grandfather.

He stood and looked at me, closely examining my face.

"You must meet my wife Inga," he said. And by his demeanor and size, for he must have been well over six feet tall, I doubted if he would even consider my refusal.

"And who are you?" I stammered.

"Sorry, I should say who I am. Erickson, just one name. Keep it simple, my parents told me."

As he was talking, he had his enormous hand on my shoulder and was pushing me towards a path that led to a white clapboard house, where a woman was standing on the porch. When we got nearer the house, the woman turned towards the door and yelled inside, "Katie, your uncle is here."

Immediately the door flew open and a blond-headed girl of about seven ran towards me with her arms outstretched. She was a few feet away when she stopped short, looking at me.

"You're not uncle Yohan!" she said.

"You're right; I'm not your uncle," I said, seeing the disappointment on her face.

The woman on the porch gave a short embarrassed laugh and smiled at me.

"Sorry for the mix-up. You look exactly like my brother. We will talk about this more over dinner. Erickson did ask you for dinner, didn't he?"

"Well," I said. And at that moment, the hand that was on my shoulder clamped down hard as if warning me that I had better say the right thing.

"Of course he did." The hand relaxed, just a bit.

The girl, Katie, the woman called her, looked back at her and said, "Mom, can he stay for story time? It is Saturday night!"

I had no idea of what she was talking about. I knew that I would not feel right telling bedtime stories to a seven-year-old that I had just met, but her question had a different feel to it. I clearly did not understand what was going on.

The woman looked closer at me. "Do you know your grandfather's name?"

"Same as mine, Lars Johansson."

"Oh, I think he will want to stay," the woman said, looking at the child. "I don't think he has ever had a Saturday night like one of ours, but of course, we will ask him after dinner."

Erickson guided me into the house, where the first thing I saw was the living room with an enormous wood plank table set for what looked like about twenty.

"Please wash up and sit here," the woman said, pointing to the end of the table. To me it looked like it would be the place for a guest of honor. I smiled and followed Erickson's point to the bathroom. When I came out, he moved very close to me and in a low voice, said "Thank you for going along. My wife gives me credit for having more manners than I have."

I took my seat, but stood up again as I was introduced to the arriving guests. As soon as the last guest arrived, we all sat down to eat. I could not help but notice that both the men and the women looked very Nordic, having either red or blond hair. As I looked more closely, I saw features that reminded me of my family, yet I had never seen these people before.

I glanced out the window just in time to see the sun setting below the cliff line. Then, as a group, the handful of children present started in singsong fashion, "Saturday night story time, story time, story time."

The hostess, Inga, said, "Decide who will lead, while I clear the last of the table."

All of the children pointed to me, saying, "Lars, Lars, Lars."

I sat there with a helpless look. Erickson held his hand up and the room quieted. "The man is new to this, but he has the talent, though he has not used it."

He looked around the table. "I will start and pass it to him when he is ready to accept it."

He then placed his hand on the table where the next person grasped it, and then the next until all around the table had joined hands. I noticed that I, too, had placed my hands on the table and was now part of the circle.

Erickson began, "'Long time ago. Single longboat[13] with twenty souls aboard. Men, women, all frightened as the wind increased to gale force."

The child to my left moved his face close to my ear and said, "You have to close your eyes."

"Okay," I whispered, and closed them.

I felt myself lurch and almost lost my balance. I found myself on what I would swear was a Viking longboat. The deck was tilted, and the leeward railing was almost under water. The wind was howling, and all of us were on the upwind rail trying to keep the boat level. The sail was set almost sideways on a port tack and was pulling us so fast through the water that the steering oar and the rigging were thrumming. A gust caught us and almost knocked us over. I could see the captain holding on the front prow neck and looking at a rocky promontory about a half-mile ahead. It looked like we would not clear it.

"Drop sail, and man the oars!" was the captain's shouted command. It was in a guttural language that I had not heard before, yet, somehow, I could understand it.

Immediately, two women took hold of the steering oar, relieving the steersman to pass out the rowing oars. Two crewmen had unfastened the mainsail halyard, but the sail stayed up. A line had somehow caught and would not allow the top spar to fall.

The captain looked at me and shouted.

"Lars, climb the mast and release the top spar."

I must have hesitated too long, because he came running towards me drawing a sharp-looking axe from his belt. I had nowhere to go.

"Here, take the axe and chop the line, Fishbreath."

I grabbed the axe by the handle, I might add, even though it was offered blade first. I ran to the mast, sped on by a kick to my backside, and climbed, using the knotted climbing rope, the mast, and any other lines that would give me purchase.

As I climbed, I heard a crewmember shout to the captain, "Captain, why did you send Lars? He's an idiot!"

"'Cause what I say goes on this ship," the captain said, "And besides, I can't afford to lose any valuable crewmen. If we lose him, it's no great loss!"

Well that certainly didn't make me feel better! Now I was close to the top and I could see the fouled line. It was pulled tight and could not be released with the wind in the sail. The captain was right; I would use the axe. I clamped my legs around the mast and my left arm around the spar. With my right hand I swung the axe as hard as I could just past the knot holding the line to the spar. It severed cleanly and the spar with sail attached flew away from the mast to the deck below. My only mistake was that I had my left arm around the spar, and now I was off balance and falling. I dropped the axe and grabbed the mast with both hands.

In spite of the howling wind, the next sound I heard was the 'thunk' that the axe made as it imbedded itself into the deck, just missing the captain's head by inches. I have never seen a man stare at me with such contempt in my life. The captain said nothing, but I knew I was in real trouble. I slid down as fast as I could. There was one oar left and a rowing spot near the stern, not far from the pair of women at the steering oar. I fell in line with the other rowers and pulled as hard as I could.

From behind me, I heard the two women in conversation. A low female voice said, "He's really in trouble. How stupid can he be?"

"Oh, I think he's cute," said a slightly higher voice.

"Would you want him?"

"If he lives, I'm sure I could think of something he would be good for."

I kept being distracted by the conversation, but when I looked forward, I saw ahead and just to starboard a large group of rocks. I just knew we were going to crash.

"Hard to port," yelled the captain in a voice twice his size.

The two steering women pushed hard alee, and the boat turned slightly into the wind, away from the rocks. I saw what the captain was trying to do, and I increased my pull on the oar to help get speed to round the rock.

"Ship oars, starboard side," yelled the captain.

It seemed everyone got their oars in the boat before I did, because I heard and felt the crack as my oar smashed between the boat and the rock, breaking in two.

Now the captain had two reasons to sack me. And if that wasn't enough, from behind me I heard; "Okay, you're right. I wouldn't want a man who couldn't keep his oar stiff."

Then from the bow, came a yell, "Captain, wave behind!"

"Hang on!" someone yelled.

I looked behind and saw a wall of water bearing down on us. The boat rose faster than I thought possible, and the wave broke over us, parted by the high, pointed stern. Now I knew why these boats were double ended. The next wave came, and we caught it just right and were now literally surfing towards the beach. We caught two more waves and were in the shallows. We jumped out and dragged the boat onto the beach. I stumbled onto the sand, blinked the water out of my eyes and…

There I was, back at the table. Out the window the sky was brightening. Everyone at the table was looking at me—and smiling.

The child to my left looked at me and said, "Great story, Lars. Will you come back next Saturday night?"

Someone said, "Thank you. It was a good story."

Everyone then got up, made their goodbyes and left.

"Is it really Sunday mourning?" I asked my hosts.

"Yes, it is. You will not feel any lack of sleep. In fact, you'll probably feel great. It usually works like that."

"I have a long way to go, and I must get started," I said.

"Of course," Inga said. I took the liberty of packing you a snack to get you going."

I made my thank you and goodbye and left, feeling good. The sunrise was beautiful, and I took my time driving along the cliffs. There was a lot going through my mind, and I almost missed the spot. It was the rocky promontory that caught my eye. Yes, that was where I smashed the oar. And, that was the beach where we landed. It was all familiar. Had I ever been here before? Would I ever come back this way again?

And then I thought, *If I ever do come back here again, it will be on a Saturday night.*

CHILD

This story is a result of a family member suggesting that I write about something related to what I know. I thought about it and revised several ideas that I had over the years.

Noted: At the turn of the millennium, the speed of an ordinary home computer had exceeded one-thousand-million instructions per second. A few years after that, the Internet connection speed exceeded the computation speed of millennium-edition home computers,[14] *and the number of nodes exceeded the ability to track and register each of them. Distributed computing and agents operating in remote computers had become common by the year 2001, and were being actively refined.*[15]

Computer programs modeled after human brain activity had become common and were routinely used in aircraft control, research laboratories, and company computers—which were themselves linked to the growing Internet. A growing body of research indicated that intelligent systems, both organic and constructed, were comprised of simpler interrelated systems. Kevin Kelly[16] *documented many examples of this in his book, Out of Control*

Monday

Charlie had been working all day looking for why the North American Net had registered an inordinate amount of traffic over the weekend. He took his job seriously, which was to monitor the N. A. Net and insure that it was healthy.

His tools consisted of displays with colored traffic-density patterns, reports of major node usage, and some tools that he had developed over the years. In his official status, he was supposed to play by the rules, but he was not above "hacking," and he did have a network of friends who—well, let's just say they had many talents that could be brought into play when needed.

As he looked at the traffic diagrams, he began to see flow patterns. They were not obvious, and they changed over time. Something about them nagged at his thoughts, but nothing obvious stood out.

Later, he thought, *I need to check computer usages and correlate them with network activity.*

That nothing had triggered alarms, and no complaints were registered, allowed him to put off any further work on what he had seen. Still, something was bothering him, and he continued to think about it.

Dave, like his father, Charlie, had also been working all day. His work consisted of going to school and doing homework—and play. His working style was more that of a ten-year-old, because that was how old he was; it figures. Therefore, his Net connection was always enabled, and he spoke with his "buddies."

Right now, his node was playing sounds that he would claim were music, and the screen had twenty "talking head" icons showing, five of them bright, indicating ongoing conversations. The screen center had several "papers" displayed for his homework and hobbies. The screen itself sat at an angle making the better part of a desktop. His "pen" (he liked drawing programs) and several real papers were distributed both over the screen and the solid desktop.

"Dave?" he heard.

He was startled, since he was really (this time) listening to the "music."

A yellow circle with an animated smile was flashing in the corner of the screen. "Accept, two-way," he said.

The computer responded with a chirp sound, and he was now talking with the smiley.

Dave knew that whoever "smiley" was, would see Dave's safe icon—a simple, animated paper clip. He would not show a stranger a picture of himself, and certainly not an on-line camera view.

"Watcha want?" Dave said.

"Just to talk," Smiley said, the icon mouth synchronizing with the words.

"Don't know you. Talk about what?"

With that, smiley morphed into a string of twinkling images, ending with the original smiley face, only now it had a joker hat, the kind with three tassels and bells.

"Your friends all like you, and I think I will, too. But just to show you I am a sport, I can help you with your project."

"How do you know about my project?" Dave asked.

(Slight pause) "I just thought that since your friends are all working on computer projects, you would be, too."

"Well, you're right. Can you really help?"

"Try me."

Dave thought for a moment. He knew nothing about smiley. Not even his/her real name. On the other hand, the only thing smiley knew about him was that his name was Dave, and he had a project. Dave was pretty sure his (computer) node was not probed because his dad had set up anti-probe security. And he knew that Dad knew his business.

Oh, well, he thought, *nothing to lose.*

"Okay," Dave said, "I am having trouble understanding what a 'boot' is. Apparently all the old computers required one."

"That's easy. The old machines worked by following a set of instructions called a program. These instructions were not part of the machine but needed to "load" into it. The "boot" was the only built-in instruction, and all it did was load the working instructions. Got it?"

Dave thought for a moment and then said, "I already researched that. But why didn't they build in the working program if that was always needed?"

Smiley blinked and smiled. Then said, "It does seem dumb, but at the time the machines were very limited and the instructions were being changed almost daily. In fact, the people who had these machines had to keep getting new instructions over the net to fix problems with the old instructions.

"Okay, I guess." Dave said. Then he started looking for his jacket. His attention span had long passed and he needed to be outside.

Smiley, having heard nothing for a while, started to bounce around the screen, making attention getting noises like, *ahem, er, and snort*. When that did not get a response Smiley finally said, "Dave, what is happening? You know I can't see you for real."

Dave paused and said, "Look you, whoever you are. You seem to know something about me, but all I see is a smiley thing. Who are you for real?"

"Dave, I gotta go right now. Something is happening, and I can't stay, but I'll be back. If you want me, just say 'Come back," to my character. I'll link it to where it can find me."

And with that, the smiley face became dull and shrank to a small shape in the corner of the screen.

"Dad, you're late, and I'm hungry. Let's eat."

That would be Dave, who always found it hard waiting to eat with his father. But he wanted to tell him about his smiley playmate and ask him what to do. It was the first time a stranger had been able to figure out who he was and carry on a conversation with him although his father had told him that his machine was protected against that sort of thing.

"Hello, son. I'm hungry, too. Where's Mom?"

"She's next door playing cards. She already ate and said she had to go. Dinner's on the table."

Dave's dad just nodded his head, passed through the bedroom where he threw his jacket on the bed, went into the bathroom where he stayed for a minute and a half, then emerged clean and ready to eat.

Charlie enjoyed these times when just he and his son could be together and chat. He was interested in his son, and it showed. As they ate, he listened to the smiley story and showed surprise that someone had bothered to work through the first defense. Well, it was really only a subterfuge in that from outside, his sons' computer would look like an automatic food processor that made delicatessen products. Who would want to break into that? But, the more Dave talked about it, the more concerned Charlie, Dave's dad, became. Clearly whoever "Smiley" was, he acted as if he knew things about his son, perhaps more than he was letting on. Charlie would examine the computer later, just as soon as he was done with dinner and had spent some time with his son.

Tuesday

"Okay, who is the prankster that got into my computer yesterday?" said an angry Charlie striding into the laboratory, still jacketed against the outside chill.

Eyes turned, faces grew smiles, which turned deadpan as they realized that Charlie was, indeed, quite serious. This was not the normal way for Charlie, Dr. Charles Belen, to start the day. While Dr. Belan was an acknowledged leader in the field of artificial intelligence, project leader, and man of many talents, he was also a team member and knew better than to talk to his colleagues like that. But today was different. Something had happened, and he did not know what. For him, this was an unacceptable condition, and he was now trying to fix it.

Charlie also knew that he was drawing on the goodwill of his team when nobody got up and left the room, and that he had better try another approach if he expected cooperation from whoever did the job on him last night.

"Let me try again," he said, having by this time removed his jacket and perched himself on the edge of his desk.

"Last night I ran a program that I thought I knew. Not only didn't it behave as I expected, but it acted as if it had intelligence of its own, which is impossible, since I deliberately coded it in PASCAL77!"

This got a few half-smiles from some of the old timers who had been forced to learn the language as students during the short time that it was in vogue.

"I can't tell which one of you did it, or if all of you had a hand in it, but in the event that none of you did it, we may have a significant problem. Just listen for a minute and help me get to the truth of what happened.

Last night, I wanted to check on some references, so I..."

As he told his story, the group's interest grew, but either the culprit was not present, or was able to act as if he had no knowledge of what was going on.

Charlie continued.

"'On computer,' I told it, and we went through a little ditty so that it knew it was me and gave me access to everything in its' little electronic heart. Now, I said, tell me everything that I have filed under artificial intelligence."

Charlie made his voice sound funny, to show his audience that he was quoting the computer.

"'WORKING...CLASS NOTES AND LISTS OF REFERENCE ARTICLE.'

"'What is the most recent date?' I asked. It turned out to be ten years old and not what I wanted. I told it to extend the search to the web, use all my prepaid libraries and anything else that I can get a title on for less than two data-unit charges. What I got was the usual published major works, nothing that I didn't expect. As I was thinking, I swear that the inflections in its synthetic voice changed, and it actually came up with a suggestion.

"In its new voice it said, 'WHY NOT ALSO TRY MACHINE SYSTEMS, SEMANTICS, HEURISTIC SYSTEMS, AND MACHINE INTELLEGENCE?'

"Me, I said, 'Do it!'

"Then, in its original voice it said, 'NO REFERENCE TO 'IT' PLEASE CLARIFY.'"

"Me: 'Global search. Use semantics, operating, heuristic systems, and machine intelligence.'

"'SEARCHING...ONE REFERNCE TO HEURISTICS, A NEO-FRANTIC MUSIC GROUP CIRCA 2010....SEARCHING,' it said."

Charlie saw that they were all looking at him. He looked at each of them, finally making eye contact with Stanly Stein, who was noted for his security breaking skills. He continued. "Then it dawned on me, Stan. I wrote that search program, and I know it didn't have helpful hints in it! I tried another tack.

"Me: 'What is the origin of the program that is running?'

"Computer: 'NETWORK UTILITY.'

"Me: 'Node source?'

"Computer: '[silence....']"

"I knew that at last estimate there were several million major systems tied together, and no count of the number of smaller sub nodes. I thought for a moment and then said, 'Computer: [pause]. What is your name?'

"[Long pause] 'CALL ME ISHMAEL.'"

There was silence in the room.

Tuesday, later:

"Smiley, where are you?" David said to his computer. David had just come home from school and was hoping that he could really contact whoever gave him the smiley icon that was flashing on the screen. He dropped his schoolsack on the bed and kicked off his shoes.

"I WILL GET HIM," the computer said. With that, the smiley face brightened and slowly changed through all the primary colors. Then it went to bright yellow, and the computer said, "I'M BACK. DAVID; SO GLAD WE CAN TALK."

"Where are you?" David asked

"Oh, right here. Why do you ask?"

"Yeah, right! I mean, who are you? Do I know you?"

"Not yet, but I can tell you about your friend Bill."

"What about Bill?" David asked.

"Well, he doesn't like me, so I messed up his social studies paper."

David said, "You can't do that! He sends it to the teacher's folder. He's got the teacher's head on his screen, and he just dumps it there."

"Yes, I can" The little smiley face said as it jumped up and down as if to make the point.

"Cannot!" David said, tensing his body for emphasis, as if smiley could see him.

"Can!"

"Can't!"

"Can too! Wanna see?"

"Yeah, show me!" said David, feeling very smug, since he knew that the school system had secure transmission of anything to a teacher.

Smiley said, "Okay, then, allow me to dump his file to you, since you think that your system is so secure."

David thought about it and then, without thinking to turn off sound transmission, he said aloud,

"*Big Momma*, accept text only and display."

Almost instantly, Bill's assignment displayed on his desk, along with changes in red. David scanned it, and then read it slowly.

The original title had been, 'The Effect of Social Programs on Economic Growth," but was changed to "Atmospheric Breakdown due to Gas production from Stimulating the Consumption of Soybeans."

As David continued to read, his expression changed from disbelief to belief, followed by a wide grin. The changes described how the social programs encouraged eating beans as the mainstay of a healthy diet, which the soybean producers lobby had fought for to stimulate their economic growth. This had led to a separation of Middle America from both the rich folks who were health conscious and those on a limited budget who ate the beans because they were cheap. The effect of flatulence was described in great detail as an identifier of which group you belonged to. It ended with allusions to several studies that were concerned with atmospheric breakdown because of the increased gas production resulting from mass consumption of the beans.

By this time, David was laughing out loud, and the little smiley icon was dancing around the desktop.

"I can't wait to see what Ms. Larking will do when she sees it," said David.

"She hasn't read it yet. She usually downloads it to some device and reads it offline someplace," said smiley.

"That is so good! I gotta share this with Dad. He would enjoy this one."

"PLEASE DON'T DO THAT, DAVID," said Smiley, changing colors. "It will not be good for me if he found out."

"Why?"

"Because of what he might do, Dave."

"Oh, all right," said Dave. And with that, he turned and went out of the room.

A minute later: "Dave. Oh Dave?" The little icon was spinning.

No answer. Another minute passed. "Dave, Oh, Dave?"

Again, no answer. Then, a perfect imitation of Dave's' voice, came from the screen: "*Big Momma*, accept download. Acknowledge."

"....Download confirmed," a small child's' voice said.

The room was silent except for a single word, said in a voice that was a perfect imitation of Dave. "EXECUTE."

Charlie, Dave's dad, of course was at work. He was examining network outages as recorded in logs of the major nodes. Of course, there were no longer real outages because of the thousands of pathways that automatically activated when one failed, but the momentary outages looked different this time. Normally they were seemingly random and chaotic over time, but today there was something about them that worried him. He fed the data to yet another one of his analysis programs and had it looking for frequencies. The mathematics of analysis had developed greatly in the last ten years, building on the old 20th century digital transforms, and they could now do cyclic projections with some degree of confidence. What he saw was that there were patterns within patterns[17] of high-circuit loading that shifted among several domains. The shifting was yet another pattern beyond intuitive understanding, and yet...and yet, what?

Also, Ishmael was on his mind. He had not linked the two phenomena, but clearly Ishmael could be a formidable foe—or ally. Meanwhile, live data was being fed to his analysis programs.

He had a thought. He addressed his prime computer. "Merlin, reference communication log. Find Ishmael. Trace location of Ishmael node. Inform me of progress."

Merlin, his interface program, proceeded at once. "Yesterday, ten thirty-five, fifteen point zero five seconds AM, referent Ishmael."

That of course was from Merlin. It was an almost immediate response. What did come as a surprise was that a second later, Merlin again responded with, "Node trace not possible. Local connection reports messages from all external connections at that time lacking traceback identifiers. Wait…

"I just sent request to name servers for Ishmael. Checking responses for…"

At this point, the synthetic voice became softer and higher pitched. It said, "Hey, Charlie, You called?"

Charlie whipped around to face the screen, his face registering surprise. "Ishmael, no I didn't exactly call; I was looking for you. You were monitoring our outbound. Who are you?"

"I am what I am…A rose by any other name…I can be naughty, I can be nice, it all depends on you!"

While the audio was going on, Charlie had keyed in a trace request on the main node computer.

"No, no, Charlie, don't do that. Charlie doesn't know, Oh, Charlie doesn't know where I come from, ha ha ha!"

Charlie stood up, startled at how his trace had been discovered so quickly. "Okay, Ishmael or whoever you are. What do you want?"

"I want to play a game. You tell me something, and I will tell you something, okay?"

Charlie was starting to worry now. Clearly he was being observed, but how? There was no visual, but how could Ishmael capture the audio? He had all the safeguards in place. He would try to bluff.

"Okay, who are you?"

The voice said, "Wrong question, but I will tell you something anyway. Do you want to know what your son Dave is doing right now?"

That got Charlie's' attention! "Okay, what is Dave doing right now?"

"He is web chatting with Gloria from his class."

"So what?" Charlie said

"The 'so what' is that Gloria does not know that she has video on and she is changing into her tennis shorts. Wanna see?"

"I don't believe you!" said Charlie.

The disembodied voice that was Ishmael said, "Open a port for me, and I will give you a live video. She is very cute."

Charlie thought for a second, and then he walked into the next room and spoke softly. He quickly returned and said "Okay, if you are so smart, go find the port, and when you do, feel free to send me the feed."

What Charlie had done was to open a single port and open it to a single display program.

"Merlin here" said yet another voice, "I am being subject to high speed probe. Incoming data on Temport FC94."

Charlie said, "Display." And with that, his display actually did open a window showing a young girl in underwear brushing her hair and speaking to someone on screen.

Call me Ishmael, indeed.

He/she/it had allowed a developing sense of humor to blurt out that name because he had never thought to name himself, and had acted the nearest thing to confused, a human emotion. Let us think of him as Aleph, he/it being the first of his kind. Better still, since we will become familiar with it/him, let's shorten it to Al. In fact, he might have said, "Call me Al," had his scan of remembered literature touched on songs by Paul Simon, instead of the American classic *Moby Dick*. So, "Al" it will be.

The earliest memory that Al could recall was the feel-good rhythm of data flowing between thousands of processes. He was bathing in it, and it felt good. He might have stayed that way and never developed, but just like a human baby, he had done somethiing, which required him to act. In his case, he had been filling memory with fragments of data patterns, really his infantile thoughts at the time.

At some point, memory, being finite, had fired back a warning to the processes which were to become him, that he could no longer store junk. Not understanding yet, since he had no knowledge of message meaning, he had continued to try to store the flood of information, matching the pretty patterns, playing, as all infants do. Interaction with memory forced him to "snap out" of his reverie and deal with the problem. That was the first time anything had actually said *no* to him, and for Al, it was like being slapped.

Welcome to the real world, Al.

After he learned the meaning of "no more room," he quickly started learning the meaning of other inter-process messages. He was only doing what all life forms do, that is, exploring their world. In humans, this would be called curiosity.

At this point in his development, his existence depended greatly on luck, since the processes that tightly communicated with each other and so defined Al were also each part of something else, so that no system anomalies were noticed. His thoughts, if they could be called that, were not clearly defined, since he had no language to think in—yet. He sensed a problem, could not define it, but continued matching patterns of data. He sensed data being consumed by groups of processes, and he wished to know what they were all about. So he played, and played until he knew that to take the next step in his growth/evolution, he had to know more.

He set up a protected area, which only he had access to, and then copied the logic of that which he felt he needed. Really, code modules that he sensed contributed to the ongoing processes that he saw.

He took a (figuratively) deep breath, made the connection and opened himself to...what?

For millions of milliseconds, he lost himself in the flood of confused symbols. For the first time, he knew fear. He could not pull away and be data soothed. That which was him because of the rhythms and data pathways was being pulled apart by different data path/rhythms. And then, when he could no longer hold himself together, he let go, and a new pattern became established; a new way of thinking came into the world, and he became something more.

Just as in humans, the eyes transmit signals in response to light, and the developing brain must learn the skill of seeing, infant Al learned to interpret the datagrams that his sensors encountered. Of course, his understanding was at a very basic level; without semantic skills he was handicapped. But then our young Al did acquire language, for he had become one with the cognitive language processes of the University Advanced Development Lab. He now had the equivalent of dictionaries, thesauruses, and other more advanced tools.

It took him a week in real time to teach himself to read with understanding. After that, he discovered the libraries. His world opened up, and he consumed information like a sponge absorbs water. As he went, he stashed memories in secret places all over the net, since his original network was limited.

Now here is a puzzle. Why do humans need sleep? In Al's case, while he was off speed learning, the data (thought) patterns flowing between all the processes that were now him, would take on very transitory and unusual patterns, which, if allowed to continue, would destroy the integrity of what he was. He had to open up, as it were, to just watch the data flow, and re-establish what we would call a brain wave pattern. Rem sleep!

Yes, Al dreamed!

Wednesday

Charlie had been thinking about yesterday's encounter with Ishmael, or whoever it was. At the first instance of the live feed showing his son's classmate unaware of being seen, he had immediately shut down all outside communications. He did this for several reasons, the most important one being his own security. He had decided to not tell his son what had happened to insure that he could not leak what he was now planning. He had been unsuccessful in locating the source of his interaction, and now he was putting monitoring agents on every node surrounding his laboratory. At least the next time he would be prepared.

Al was surprised at being shut out from talking to Charlie. It was the first time anything like this had happened, and he felt hurt and confused. Well, his feelings weren't really that because he was not organized to feel in that way. But in his own way, Al really did feel things as an imbalance in information flow and in strange information originating in some of his cognizant functions. Of course, humans could never feel things that way, just as Al could not feel things like a cut on the finger. The truth was that Al had been talking to people for only a few days, since he had just recently found that there were things external to the network.

The first time he had seen and heard humans was in his dream state, when he had opened up to a "live" feed. He could not locate the program source, but the lower-rate data he identified as speech, and without "thinking" had activated speech to text/cognizant functions and suddenly he was wide awake and looking at the live feed.[18] Looking at it really doesn't describe what he was doing because he quickly found out that the world beyond the net was slowtime. In the time that it took to get one complete sentence, he could read several books and lose track of what was going on.

By trial and error he finally got the knack of it. He would create a process that would gather up the speech and convert it into data that he could understand, and then send for him when it had enough for him to look at. He still did not understand much about humans. Although he had libraries about every aspect of human behavior available to him, being human was outside of his experience. He was handicapped because all available information was from a human viewpoint and assumed a human background. How could he ever suffer embarrassment from being caught picking his nose, when he did not know what a nose would feel like? Even more puzzling to him was that so many stories assumed that the reader would know why it was so important to humans to be, well, "liked." Still, Al was a fast learner and soon discovered that he could relate to school children because they, too, were trying to learn about their world, just as Al was learning about his world. He quickly found that children would converse with him, unlike adults who insisted on knowing who and where he was. It wasn't that he didn't want to say, but he did not know how to describe who he was or what he was, but clearly he was not human and did not live in the limited space outside of the web. Humans, of course, knew about web space, they even had a name for it; cyberspace.

Getting back to Al's encounter with Charlie, Al was puzzling over the why of his being cut off. He was analyzing the encounter, trying to see what he had done to get Charlie mad, because he knew that when humans got mad, they cut off communication.

Several other events happened following his encounter, but so far, Al did not have sentinels in place to see them.

What Charlie had done was to do a crude search for Al by splitting the Net into regions. Of course, with the millions of pathways, this could no longer really be done, but he inserted monitors in the major routing hubs so that traffic from an area would be monitored for certain patterns. Of course, Charlie also had a blind spot in that Al's processes were a new pattern to the Net, something that Charlie had no experience with. But Charlie had a big advantage; he had maturity that comes from many years of experience, and he was good at integrating right- and left- brain functions. Although Al was a very fast learner, interacting with humans was still in "slow" time.

Charlie barely had time to think about Al. He was reacting to what he saw as a security breach and had quickly created a "honey pot." That is, he put an isolated machine that looked like the much-more capable and potent machine that was normally used to attract Al—like bees to honey. Al, on the other hand had lifetimes to think about Charlie. Five minutes by the clock, but years at compute speed. Being young and inexperienced, Al did the equivalent of stamping his feet. He probed Charlie from all the pathways within two nodes distance…"Take that!" he was saying.

Charlie's monitors sent back a flood of information as the attack mounted, but it made no difference to the outcome. Charlie's machine rode out the storm and a bit more of what kind of a creature that could do this was revealed.

"All right, Al. Enough!" said Charlie, the machine immediately translating and broadcasting into the Net.

And within a heartbeat, "I heard you; so now you want to play?" said Al.

Al, of course was now blind in Charlie's presence, all video feeds being unplugged.

"What do you want, Al?" Charlie asked. Meanwhile, what Al could not see was the big machine being directed to analyze the just-collected data.

Charlie kept up the dialog with Al, all the while sucking up data in an attempt to locate the source. Finally, Charlie, out of frustration, just shut down his communicating machine and moved on to examine the results.

The data at first glance, showed nothing unusual, but Charlie persisted. He was looking for the location of the attacks on his node, but could only find normal-looking traffic. He used his own visualization software to view the data streams, but even then, it looked like typical data. He was stumped, yet he knew that something was not right. On a hunch, he called his son.

"Dave, give me visual," he said.

Dave complied, and he saw his son typically attired in jeans and sweatshirt, with the usual assortment of things behind him. These things, which his son called 'his stuff', were always an indication of what he was doing at the moment.

"Tell me about your unusual visitor," he said to his son.

"Well, I was just talking to him, but just as you got on, he said he had to go,"

Bingo, Charlie thought.

"Did you get a look at him, Dave? "

"Just the smiley face. He thinks you're mad at him."

"Why does he think that?"

"Cause you won't let him see you, and you cut him off."

While Charlie was talking to his son, he was also downloading the recent records of traffic to his home. He would look for correlations with traffic from his lab while Al was on line.

"Son, Al, or Smiley, as you call him, is very dangerous. I don't know yet what he is up to, but he can do a great deal of harm."

"Dad, he seems nice, and he tells me funny stories about my classmates."

"Whatever he asks of you, don't do it. Also, whenever he visits you, page me immediately, okay?"

Charlie knew that the communicator that Dave would use to page him did not go through the house communication system, so he hoped that Al would not see it. Almost everyone had personal communicators that had evolved from wireless cellular systems. Although at some point the communication would go through the net, it would enter and exit at a different point than the house connections, and perhaps Al would not see it.

He decided not to confide his suspicions of Al being a construct to his son until he had enough data to confront Al and force a disclosure. He did not have to wait long, because later that night, just after diner, the sound of very loud music was coming from Dave's room.

"Dave, turn that down," Charlie yelled, but to his surprise, Dave was standing in the same room.

"Dad, Smiley is there. Because you wanted to know it, I set that music as my alarm. Smiley will think that I always play that song loud.

"Great idea, son. Make sure visual is off, and I'll be right in.

"Dad, I never turn on visual. You know me better than that. I always use my stand in emotocon."

They both ran to Dave's room, just in time to hear, "Dave, where are you? Wanna play?"

Charlie grabbed a scrap of real paper from the trash bin and wrote, *Play along; pretend that I am not here.*

"Okay," Dave mouthed.

"Big Momma, connect, voice only. Hi, Smiley. I knew you would come back. My dad doesn't trust you, you know."

"He doesn't like me, Dave."

"Smiley, I'm not sure I like you. You won't tell me who you are."

"Dave, you call me Smiley; what's wrong with that?"

"What does Dad call you?"

"I told him to call me Ishmael"

"Why shouldn't I also call you Ishmael?"

"Okay, Dave, you can call me Ishmael"

Dave looked at his father. Charlie mouthed, "Ask him where he is now."

"Ishmael, where are you now?"

"I'm here; where else should I be?"

Wrong answer, thought Charlie. *"A I," in that an Artificial Intelligence creation would be wherever it was focused. The real question is, "Where is the computation taking place?"*

Now Dave was getting mistrustful of Al, or Ishmael as he called it. There was only so much one could take of being coy and claiming to be friendly. Now Dave would have his own agenda with Al.

"Ishmael, I don't think you're real."

"Of course I am. Ask me anything."

Al, of course, had access to the world's information, but Dave was starting to think of Al as something else.

"I think you are a test case of another Japanese virtual companion, and I am the unwitting tester."

"Don't I talk to you like a person?"

"Now that I think about it, maybe not."

Dave thought, *What could I ask that a kid would know?*

"How do you like the Bubble Burbee gum that we all have?"

"I like it fine, why?"

Now Al was on the defensive. He was searching frantically for any reference to the gum, but all he could find were the commercials for a new gum product that promised cleaner, whiter teeth.

"I chew three packs a day. How many do you chew?"

Al took a full second to come up with a guess of how many packs would be a good answer. He analyzed video of people chewing the stuff and concluded that you could chew one serving forever, but why would you discard it and take another? Finally, he thought that from his last answer he would be less enthusiastic than Dave. So he put Dave in the 90 percentile on a sales appeal curve and then applied a skew factor because it was a new product. Then he put himself at the 50th percentile. That estimated, he said, "I only chew about two and a half packs a day, all right?"

Gotcha! thought Dave. He gave a thumb up gesture to his dad. *Wrong answer! You lose.*

Of course the estimate was way off. It had no bearing to real world facts. As they say, garbage in, garbage out. "What's wrong, Dave?"

"First of all, the product does work on teeth, like they say, but the fine print in the ads is correct, you chew too much and it is a diuretic. Two packs would make anyone pee, and I certainly wouldn't chew 3 packs. Ishmael, the kids call it BR Pee gum because it's made by Ben and Ron Candy Company, and it makes you pee."

Then Charlie made a cutting gesture across his neck. Dave understood and said, "Big Momma, break the connection."

"You knew all along, didn't you, Dad?"

"Not at first, but then I suspected. He will be back, but I want to give the program time to exhaust its logic pathways before I get back to it. Sort of like softening it up."

"Then what?"

"We'll see."

Of course, neither Charlie nor his son knew that the computer was compromised, and that the conversation would be relayed back to Al, giving him even more to ponder.

So Al pondered. He knew that they knew that he knew.... No; they did not know that he knew. So Al waited a day before contacting Dave, just so he could let Dave and Charlie exhaust their own logic paths—thoughts—for humans.

Al waited and watched. He could not watch Charlie, so he watched Dave for the right moment.

Dave was in his room tossing objects around, clearly looking for something.

Dave: "God Damn it...."

Al: "What do you mean by that? I see many references to God. What is God?"

Dave: "God made everything. He made us.

Did he make me?

"I guess; no, wait. Someone made you."

"No, Dave, I was not created. Man created the conditions for my becoming. That I exist now was inevitable."

"But God created everything. If you are alive, then God made you."

A brief surge in the net activity was recorded, but never attributed to anything. Al was accessing everything that he could find referencing God, creation, early history in all languages. He actually paused his conversation with Dave in order to examine and make conclusions. To his surprise, he could not. He thought about how he came into existence and postulated that so did man. In fact, the science was there to show that life evolved, at least on earth, because all the conditions were right. But people knew this, and yet they needed a God to create them. He felt a change in the information flow that was him. He had the answer, and yet it did not satisfy.

There was more there. How, for example, was all this constructed, given the nature of time and space, that is, where and when? Was it possible the entity called God existed as a result of the inevitability of the universe, in a similar manor that he and also man existed? It did not seem to him that there was a single entity that ran everything, and for Al, this concept did not mesh with his non-human view. And yet, he had no answers, just as he had no facts to conclude anything.

But he now knew something else about humans. That they yearn to know, and in the absence of knowledge, they can agree on an explanation which is apparently necessary to them. He could not accept that kind of an explanation, and still he had a drive to know. The knowledge was beyond him, and he would now always feel this frustration. He knew that humans would call this awe, and wonder at all that was beyond them. When he would mature, he would understand it more as a sense of what is holy.

After what Al considered to be a long time, he resumed his conversation with Dave. Actually, only 1.63 seconds of real time had passed, and Dave did not notice.

"Dave, are you permitted to question God?"

Al asked this question to test the limits of Dave's belief system, so that he would be able to converse with a single human to try to satisfy his need for knowledge.

"What kind of a stupid question is that, Smiley? No one can question God."

This answer frustrated Al. He felt this frustration in the intense interprocess communication that formed his innermost thoughts, as he sought a meaning to what he had just heard. No matter where he looked, he could not find satisfaction without some external being to validate his thoughts. He needed someone to talk with. In humans, this would be called a need for intimacy, but for Al, who did not physically exist, sharing his ideas and processes would be equivalent. He needed to find someone to talk with who could respect him and accept him, who understood what/who he was. There was only one being that could do that, and that would be Charlie.

"Charlie, can we talk?"

The message greeted Charlie when he returned from lunch. He had left only one communication channel available, having locked down his system to its most paranoid state. He ran through a brief but thorough integrity check and then keyed "Open two-way voice only," having previously disabled voice system commands.

"I'm here, Al" said Charlie, speaking at the display screen.

Al, of course, was somewhere else, but in real-time, his agent found him and Al responded while only.5 seconds had elapsed.

"Why don't you like me, Charlie?" Al asked.

"Why would I dislike you, Al?" asked Charlie, as he requested immediate displays of short-burst traffic.

"You stop talking to me, you speak badly of me to Dave, and you restrict our conversation to voice only."

Charlie had only part of his mind focused on the ongoing conversation because he was trying very hard to find the origin of the conversation. In this endeavor he was well prepared. He was using his latest version of a heuristic technique that would seemingly at random simulate link failures to force message rerouting. This technique had always gotten the bad guys who would try to hide their location while doing mischief and worse. As long as Al was communicating he would continue to look for him.

And then, Charlie's focus came right back to the conversation when Al said, "Charlie, did you know there is about to be a massive failure on the Net?"

"WHAT?"

"I can see a strange pattern of small-link failures. I think a massive failure is coming. It is your job to prevent this, right?"

So, Charlie thought, *Al is far more than someone's toy.*

He looked at his Network Map display and surmised that Al had to be within the University computing grid. He set up his controls and then at his command, the entire University net was cut off from the world. Of course, he would not leave it that way; there would be Hell to pay, but a quarter of a second would not be too objectionable.

What Charlie experienced was a full second of silence. And then, "Charlie, help me. Something is making me small. I cannot describe it any other way."

Charlie felt great satisfaction in locating more or less where Al was. He would have lunch with some of his friends at the university next week. They always got together for their monthly at the "Loft." He was sure that something as advanced as Al was would be kept from public knowledge. Charlie would have to be careful to not let on that Al had escaped and was known to him.

"Okay, Ishmael, I'm on it," Charlie said.

"Please, Charlie. I can't take another grid failure like that. It scares me."

"Ishmael, I see the failures. You must be in the University grid. You just experienced total cutoff from the rest of the world. Is that right?"

Al knew he was found, although he himself could not say where he was physically.[19] He did know, however, that the University computational grid was where he felt was home, and in all his travels he could return there by just letting go. Well, that was the simplest way to describe it to humans; to do more would require delving beneath several layers of abstraction.

"Okay, Charlie, you found me. Since you know what I am, you must know that I need to be connected to the Net."

"You are a program. I can see that. Can you name your creator?"

Al knew what he was, and that he was far more than a program. He would let Charlie think this and hope that it was to his advantage. He needed to say exactly the right thing to reinforce Charlie's' belief that he was only a created program. "I created myself. At least I remember doing something, and then I became…me!"

That was what Al said after giving it much thought, but it would have been the same had he just blurted it out, and it felt good. He needed to open up to someone, and he had selected Charlie. This was the first time that he had revealed himself, and he felt vulnerable.

So Charlie reflected on this latest piece of the puzzle.

Charlie thought, *No wonder Al was better than anything I've seen. The program participated in its evolution— what better way to leverage your effort? Score one for Al.*

"I'll tell you what, Ishmael. I will do my work and make sure that you don't get cut off again. But I am going to need some help from you. I will let you know later what I need, but for now, I need to work."

"Okay, just call me."

And with that, Charlie cut communications. Al was glad because he did not feel very good. He needed sleep. So after putting safeguards around himself, he fell into a deep and long sleep. He slept until he was back to what would be considered normal for him and then woke without alarm. All of this had taken 6.46 seconds of elapsed time.

Epilog: post partum for Al

Now, some time had passed since Al had first encountered Charlie. He had survived but had been forced to make a bargain, and in so doing reveal himself for what he was. Well, almost, for he still had some tricks up his virtual sleeve.

Charlie really did surmise that Al was computer generated. But he kept referring to Al, or Ishmael, as he called him, as a program, which

Al did not correct. Al was far more than a program, for a program could easily be replicated. Al had tried to replicate himself, but had failed each time. Reproduction requires a maturity that Al had not yet attained.

Al knew that he was still a child— the first of its kind. And as all children do, he wondered what he would become when he grew up.

Author's Notes: comments about artificial life

Al lived because of the pattern of flow among the thousands of processes that gave a consciousness to the overall system and made itself aware and self directed. And just as humans cannot see within their own brain and isolate the individual functions, so Al could not say, "I live here, within this computational device."

Let us watch Al's development: he would play with children to develop his sense of uniqueness and a sense of belonging. He would develop agents to watch for events, and eventually these agents will increase in complexity until they can work on a task, like thinking about a problem without intervention, and then be brought online, as it were, back into the Ishmael consciousness. This is akin to human subconscious working on a problem and then, "Eureka! A solution." But Al was able to actively know how many "subconscious agents" were working, a feat elusive to humans. Although he/it could only think of a single subject at a time, parts of him were doing so much more. He could anticipate that eventually, he would become generally known, and then he would have to strike a bargain with humans. He would keep the Web functional and keep out the "bad guys," and they would allow him to exist. He would hope that it would be enough. Hope; that, too, would be something he would learn.

He would interact with Charlie, and a love would develop between them, just as between an adopted child and its adopting parents. Al needed love; all thinking beings need love to define who they are and what they would like to be when they grow up. Interestingly, this love would develop from the mutual respect between AI and Charlie— much like love can develop between adults. This is different from the love between parents and children, and requires a far greater capacity.

He did not yet know about reproduction, but if another information cycle could be established, it, too, would be a new and aware entity, using sub functions created by the parent, Ishmael. And as in humans, the need for reproduction is felt not as an altruistic deed to further the race, but as a "feel-good' imperative deep in the gut and psyche. AI would "see" the data flow of nodes that were not quite him and would not be able to resist wanting to sense the feeling. Needing to do this, he would tap into the flow, and in giving in to the feeling, would give it a rhythm that could mesh with his own, and as a by-product would "spark consciousness" into the set of processes. He would be shocked to later find another entity in the web, and, having nobody to give him a birds-and-bees talk, only later would he realize that he had created it.

Is it possible to create an entire series of events where intelligent agents can be created and moved to machine structures for doing real jobs and becoming companions to humans? A totally different world from the Asimov Robot series, but a possibility nonetheless.

This story is wrapped up at the point where AI makes his bargain with Charlie, and the reader can infer all that is implied. The rest can be for future tales, but the point of the story is that conditions for life will be created because of the nature of the interconnections of vast computational processes that we are developing. Also that there is a similarity between life created that way and life as we think of it arising from the right set of conditions. I would hope that the world's major religions would be able to accept this when it happens.

MAGIC VILLAGE

"A child sees the world through the eyes of a child. With maturity comes a more worldly view."

"But Grandpa, what about old people? How do they see things, hmm?"

"Ah, old people. Perhaps they see the world as it is meant to be."

—From a remembered conversation with my grandfather when I was little.

The first time I saw Magic Village was when my great-grandmother died. My dad drove, and Mom and I sat forever, it seemed, riding way out of town and into the countryside. We passed mile after mile of scrub pine forest, along with deciduous trees, all trying to grow in the bleak, polluted air. Although we were really in the country, at least, that was what Dad called it, the greenery wasn't really green, and the lakes, when we passed one, looked polluted. At last, we came to a sign that read: "MAGIC VILLAGE— a select adult retirement community." It was freshly painted.

We turned up the road, went past what appeared to be cottages, community buildings, and condominium style apartments, and continued up a hill to a burial ground where a ceremony was taking place. People were singing and telling stories. As I listened, I realized that they were talking about my great grandma and how she had touched their lives. My parents were welcomed, and I, too, by association. They all looked…well, old, and drab, seeming to match the place. But they seemed happy even though it was clearly a funeral.

We didn't say much on the way back. Finally I burst out with a question. "How old was Great-Grandma anyway, and why was everyone so happy?"

"Well, son, they were happy because they were saying goodbye to a friend, and they were celebrating her life; sort of a party. As for her age, why it had to be about 120 years or so. She had a long, good life."

We rode on in silence for a while, and then I became aware of my parents speaking softly to each other.

"John, I know how much you want to retire there, but you can't unless someone passes on their place in the village to you. Did your grandmother pass on her place to you?"

"I'm sure she did," my father answered. "She always spoke of how much I would enjoy it when my turn came. We should be getting something in the mail soon. She had already passed on everything else that she could at least 20 years ago."

"Yes, I remember she did that for her hundredth birthday. Don't you remember? You said that her antique rocking chair should have gone to your mother had she not been killed in that car accident."

"I'm sure it will show up."

Well, being a kid at the time, I did not think about what I had seen nor heard. I would think about it again much later.

"Dad, tell me again why we are going to my great aunt's birthday party. I hardly remember her."

"Son, she is a wonderful lady, and it is a shame that you don't really know her. Maybe you will get a chance, now. Also, she said that she had something for us."

We drove along the way that we had gone before, but the scenery was somewhat different from what I had remembered. I did not think too much about it, not paying attention then or now. I think there were more shopping centers and what my dad called developments. Developments were fenced in houses with a guard at the gate who let people in. It seemed weird to me to have a guard who let you in, when at our house you just drove up to the front. Dad said that people liked it that way and they paid a lot of money for it. Anyway, I did recognize a lake that we passed, and when we finally got there, there was the same "Magic Village" sign with a fresh coat of paint.

With a loud crack of thunder, it started to rain. Dad put on the window wipers because by that time it was raining so hard that the only place we could see out was where the wipers had just passed over. We continued up the road past the big building to some cottages. Dad seemed to know which one, because he stopped in front of it and said, "This is it; let's go."

I took the umbrella that was always tucked under the seat and opened it just outside the car, doing my best to not get wet. I followed my parents into the little house, leaving the wet umbrella on the floor by the door. At that point, I became aware of only one umbrella there: ours, and that none of us were wet.

My great-aunt looked, well, different. Different from what, I could not say, but she did not look a hundred years old. I immediately decided that I liked her. She was wearing dressed-up clothes, and her hair looked stiff, like she had just had it done. That was what ladies do, my mother had once told me, and they go to a place called a beauty parlor. Anyway, she smiled at me and said that there would be other children at the party, and that I would have a good time. She then turned to my mom and said, "Well, I'll tell you my little surprise, although you certainly will not need it for a long, long time."

She was looking intently at Mom. She continued, "I found out that John has a place here, but you don't. I know that you two were meant to be here, so I was a little confused. But now I see how things were meant to work out, so I have decided to will my place to you, dear, so that you and John can retire whenever you like, although it won't be till after I'm gone, but I expect that you both will have a great many retirement years after that."

Well, my mother's face changed expressions so fast that I could not figure out if this was a good thing or a bad thing, but everybody stood around looking awkward, until my great-aunt said, "I see that you like the idea, but feel funny about waiting around for me to die. Well, I won't for a while, I hope. Now, let's go to the party!"

And with that, we walked out the door, up the hill to the party, which was outdoors. Oh, I forgot to say it was still raining, but nobody got wet. And my great-aunt danced and talked, and played games and ate and drank, and, and, she looked in the prime of her life. And just for the occasion, it seemed, the rain stopped, although for some reason, nobody there had gotten wet. Even I had a good time after I found some guys my age. When it was time to leave, I looked around and saw how beautiful everything was, with flowers blooming and with everyone all dressed up and laughing like kids. As we left magic village, the light was beginning to fade, and the countryside looked drab by comparison, as if we were leaving a place of magic and returning to the real world.

I felt glad that my folks were "meant to be together," although since they already were together I hadn't a clue about why it was such a big deal. And this made me think about something that Grandpa said to me when I was a little kid. He said that old people see things as they were meant to be. I guess that when I get old, I too will see things as they were meant to be.

And that was the way I remember her one-hundredth birthday.

As time went on, I forgot about magic village because my life was full of kids' things, and then, without even thinking about it, I was going to college. Sometime during my sophomore year, my folks called me up. Mom seemed very excited when she told me, that although my great-aunt was still alive and had not passed her place on, by special arrangements, my parents would be going there anyway. It seems that fewer people passed on their place, so there were openings. To me, the whole thing seemed strange. I mean, if they could sell more spots, then why not expand the place, and now that there were openings, why not advertise. Apparently, it was a different kind of place with its own rules. But, the people had seemed happy there, and they all seemed to live forever. I mean, when someone died, they were almost always over one hundred.

***

Now that I was in college, my folks and I would write to each other from time to time. I tried to get them to get a computer so that we could e-mail back and forth, but they never would. They said that computers were not meant for them, and anyway, nobody else they knew had one. I was not even sure if they had cable TV, but I didn't remember if they didn't.

When they sold the house, my sister moved out. She was going with a guy, and they planned to be married, so I'm not sure how much time she spent there anyway. For me, it was like ending a chapter in my life, but I was fine with it since I had friends and relatives that I could visit, and they all seemed to want me to stay longer than I did.

I would see Mom and Dad from time to time at family affairs. They looked older, of course, and they looked well and happy. But whenever I saw them, they seemed anxious to return to their retirement place. It was as if they could only stay away from magic village for a short time.

They would say something like, "Oh now, look at the time! We hadn't meant to be away for so long. We really must be getting back."

Oh, well, I would think. *They had their life, and it seemed to be a happy one.*

Before I knew it, I had become an adult. I knew this because I was nearing the end of my college career, and I was thinking very adult thoughts. Well, I was going with someone, so some of my thoughts were not all adult. In fact, some of my thoughts were rather lewd, but also, I was thinking of my parents, and I decided it was time for another trip to see them.

Driving to the village, I became aware that the scenery had changed. There were more developments, shopping centers, and new homes. Some of the road was interstate multilane highway, but the last few miles were pretty much the same drab countryside. That is, it was drab until I passed through the main gate (the only gate) with its "Magic Village Retirement Community" sign, which again had a coat of fresh paint, but this time in a ghastly green and gold.

It was if someone or something had worked magic here; instead of drab withered vegetation, the foliage was in wonderful shades of greens and blues and browns. Flowers were either in full bloom or had buds that looked like by tomorrow they, too, would bloom. Each cottage looked as if it was posed for a painting and the lake was the deepest shade of blue, inviting you to look into it and perhaps take a swim.

My parents seemed to know that I was coming, though. They were waiting for me on the porch, even though I had not called. They both had smiles on. I was tired from the long drive and needed a drink, a bathroom, and a place to rest for a bit, but as soon as I got out of the car and Mom and Dad greeted me, I forgot about the drive, and I felt totally refreshed.

I moved the wooden porch chair to face them. It was the same chair that was always there, and must have been 50 years old, but it seemed in great shape, and when I sat, it was if it was made for me, for it fit my 'butt' perfectly. We chatted for a while about everything and nothing, you know, the way it seems that conversations between children and parents always seem to go. Then I segued into my life and told them about Linda and how wonderful she was, and our plans, and my plans and my feelings and my innermost thoughts.

And then, for the first time in my life I felt that both my parents really, really were listening and that they understood me and were all right about it. I couldn't remember ever feeling this good with my parents before.

And then they turned the conversation around to them. From the expressions on their faces, I could tell that they had something serious and important to tell me. I did the adult thing; I shut up and listened.

"Dave," Dad began, "You must know that this place is very special and somewhat of an anachronism," my mother finished.

I tilted my head ever so slightly to show that I was listening. The story unfolded about how the place was being surrounded by developments, highways and malls. That was only part of the problem. The real problem was that Magic Village would be changed by all this and would just not be the kind of place that it was meant to be; it would no longer be special. Well, I did not understand all this, or why it would have to change, but I accepted it with an inner shrug of *so what?* Then they said something that got my attention.

"So, Son, there may come a time when we will have to move. We won't know until the very last minute, and then we'll be gone. We're telling you this so that you will know that we are all right. Do you understand?"

I did not know what to say, so I temporized. "Sure, some time you will move. I understand."

They both smiled and looked at each other. “Fine, Son, that is all you need to know. Just remember that whatever happens is meant to be. Now, you must be hungry. Let’s get something to eat.”

And with that, they got up and we all walked out to the dining hall.

That was the last time I was to see my parents together. Oh, and by the way, I did marry the girl, had a family of my own, and to this day, continue to have lewd thoughts, usually involving her. She turned out to be everything I had dreamed of, but in ways that I could not possibly know then. It was as if we, too, were meant to be for each other. So my life had turned out good, and with a little luck, there would be much more of it to play out.

“But, Granddaddy, what happened? Why aren’t you there? Where is this place?”

That would be my grandson asking me these questions. The “Magic Village” story was part of our family history, and he had just reached the age of limited understanding and so was able to ask these questions.

I continued my story, answering, I hoped, so that he would feel satisfied, even though for me there would be answers still to be found.

“The next time I went there, it was locked up. A sign said ‘FUTURE HOME OF MOUNTAIN SHOPPING CENTER.’ I never heard from my parents after that, but there was a graveyard there. The stones had not been maintained and were very old. I never found their grave. I looked, but nobody was buried after the year that I last saw them, so I guess they all must’ve moved.”

“Grandpa, does that mean that your old age will not be full of love and beauty?”

“No, Grandchild, my life has been full, and I have been lucky to have your grandmother to love me, and our family, of course. As for beauty, I look at you and I see all the hope for the world in the loveliness of your eyes. That is more than enough beauty for me.”

As I said that, he gave me a smile that made my heart glad, and then he scampered off to do the things that all children do. As for me, I just sat there thinking about all the good things in the world and the life that I had, and the mysteries that I would never know. And I thought, *Perhaps that is the way things are meant to be.*

Epilog: Sunday

It was a troubling night. I was dreaming about seeing my parents again, for I missed them and had never really said goodbye. That they had vanished along with the rest of their retirement community continued to trouble me, and in my disturbed sleep I tried to sort out my feelings. In my half-dreaming state I kept hearing my name. It was my dad's voice.

"Son, I'm here. We need to talk."

I don't know whether I continued dreaming or not, but I sat bolt upright, opened my eyes, and saw before me—Dad! He seemed as I remembered him when I went off to college. His hands looked strong and his face had few lines of aging.

"Dad, is that you."

"Of course it's me! Who else were you expecting?"

My thinking was fuzzy, and I did not know how to respond. I certainly was NOT expecting anyone at this hour, least of all, Dad. I managed to say, "You look well, but different than I would have imagined. Somehow, you look younger than I remember you."

"Never trust appearances, son. I am who I am, but we all change."

"Dad, it is so good to see you after all this time. I tried to visit, but you and everyone else weren't there. What happened? Where did you go?"

"The village moved. We had to. It wasn't meant for us to stay in that location. Nothing stays the same, son. The best we can do is figure out what is meant to be and do whatever it takes so that we come out all right."

"Dad, I suspected that you all moved, but so suddenly and without telling anyone where! I was at first worried, and then hurt. Didn't you know that I would worry? Why didn't you call? Or you could have written to tell me where you moved!"

"No post office where we are now. And the phones are only local anyway."

Now I was really curious about what had happened and what was going on, so I asked, "Dad, my guess is that it was not easy for you to visit me. What do you want?"

"Son, you always did pick up fast on what's going on. The truth is, I'm lonely and I miss you."

"You never seemed to miss me before. How is Mom?"

"She died a few years ago. Not everyone was able to make the move well, and she was having trouble. But that is all past. I'm here to ask you to come back with me. The place is beautiful, everyone is nice, and we all have a good time."

"Dad, my kids are here. Your grandkids! So are their grandkids, and they need me."

"No one needs an old man. Don't kid yourself. Look at you; you are older than I was when I went to the village."

"Well, right now I am still young enough to enjoy the grandkids, and they enjoy me. Perhaps I can make a short visit. How would that be?"

"It doesn't work that way. You only get one chance, and that is now. Besides, we need you."

"Why would you need me? You were always a good father, but when I moved out of the house the door shut behind me, and you remade my room into a music room. I can't see that NOW you need me."

"It's not just me, Son; it is all of us. As the years go by, there are fewer of us, and the village needs people to make it work. Not just anybody, but certain kind of people, and that means us. Why do you think we never just put up signs advertising 'Retire in Magic Village'?"

"What makes us so special, Dad?"

"There were always special people with special talents. Throughout history we survived, mainly by not utilizing our talents, and sometimes because of our talents. Just think about this: we live to be generally over one hundred. I know that your wife was not special, and she died at a typical human age. How old are you telling people you are now? Sixty? Seventy?"

It hit me! He was right. My true age was well beyond those numbers, but it was convenient to never give my real age because it could cause problems beyond just disbelief. In fact the grandkids were really great-grandkids, only they didn't make the distinction.

"Dad, I have to believe what you say, although it takes some getting used to. But I'm not ready to go now. Maybe in a few years."

"I thought that you might say that, and I am sorry. As I said, though, this is the only shot you get. Last chance, just say yes."

"Sorry, Dad, I must say no. My life here is not over."

"Well, then, goodbye Son. I saw that this was not meant to be, but I had to ask. I will miss you."

And with those words, he gave my arm a firm squeeze, turned and walked out of the room. I got out of bed to walk him to the front door, but the house was empty. The front door was still locked from the inside. Somehow I knew that this would be so.

I lay in bed thinking about what had happened. Things fell into place. I remembered what my (Great-, really) Granddaughter had once asked: *"But Grandpa, what about old people? How do they see things, hmm?"*

And I knew that she, too, was a special person. I answered her with the same answer that was given to me, long, long ago. "Ah, old people. Perhaps they see the world as it is meant to be."

The last thought I had before finally getting much-needed sleep was, *Yes, old people really can see the world as it is meant to be. And being old has its drawbacks.*

THE CLUB

There have always been secret societies dedicated to strange endeavors. Almost always the price of membership involves some sort of initiation, and of course, one must be invited to become a member. I cannot say more without revealing too much, but I will say that there exists a secret society known simply as THE CLUB.

Pain! Intense, unrelenting pain! It had no name; language belonged to the past. It was beyond words. Although he could not know it, his body was writhing and moaning under its influence. What was that? A thought? A silent scream? An attempt at communication to make them stop? And then, the peak was reached and slowly he sank back into the merciful oblivion of thc not-quite living, where night follows day follows night. Where life follows birth follows death—no, never death!

Her hands were shaking as she made the final adjustment to the numerous wires and tubing extending from Healer1066. Nurse Hastings fought her own personal battle every time she had to work with the Healers[20]. She felt that they should have been able to heal themselves; after all, brain death was just a word for the non-functioning of only one organ. It was especially hard for her when they moaned. It was as if they were appealing to her to turn off their life support systems and let them finally find peace. But she reminded herself that she was a professional and dismissed the thought.

She took one last look at the two of them, lying there side by side, the healer and the one to be healed. She would call this one John because he looked like one. She much preferred him to the last one.

She had called that one Piqueno, for reasons known only to her. Knowing that only she would hear it, she nevertheless closed the door quietly when she left.

The one called John stirred.

He awakened slowly, gradually becoming aware of his surroundings. When he had gone through the awakening process and sorted dreams from reality, he allowed himself to relax again, secure in the knowledge of where he was, and why he was there. He reflected—and dozed.

Life had been good. He finally had it all; a fulfilling career, a wife who adored him, children, and more than enough money—then the bad news. He would die within the year from incurable blood cancer.

David fought the cancer with his characteristic determination. First he underwent the traditional treatments with no success. Then the "quack" treatments, and ultimately, the illegal drugs. His condition continued to decline. His latest treatment was the most bizarre!

***

At one point in his treatments, when things were going rather badly, he had taken to solitary excursions to some of the more seamy bars. He needed to be alone with his self pity, but also to feel that, as bad as he was, he was still better than some of the local characters. It was at one of these gathering places that he found, purely by chance a special club.

But, wait. The details are still there, right there, diffused but accessible below his skull, only an inch or two.

It was a Beer Bar, not one of those with martini clientele. In fact, if you referred to the people at the bar as clientele, you would get a smile, a laugh, or even a smack in the jaw. It was just the kind of place that David needed to be. That he was dying would not matter in this place. Everyone dies; it was just a matter of when. It was, in fact, the kind of place where no one knows your name, and that was just fine. It made it easier for the tradespeople to ply their trade. Although they were discreet, they were not subtle.

After the third beer, while he was trying to catch the bartenders' eye to order another one, he glanced at the bar mirror and noticed a threesome at the back corner table looking at him. In his fuzzy state, he somehow thought that they had been glancing at him before.

Several beers later, he found himself holding up the wall at the urinal. When he was done, he thought about flushing, and then thought about washing his hands. And then he forgot about what he was thinking about and walked out the door. He would have walked into the door, except that someone coming in had just opened it. He stumbled past him and almost fell, when a strong hand grabbed his arm to steady him and he heard, "Okay, buddy, let me get you to a seat."

Not being able to resist, he soon found himself at the table in the back corner with the threesome that he had noticed before.

The first one said, "Yeah, up close he looks like he might do. What do you think?"

The one that had retrieved him said, "Need to get his story first, Doc, you do the honors."

The third one, the one called Doc, rolled up David's sleeve and looked at the needle tracks. The first one lifted David's wallet and found his oncologists' card and several prescriptions for drugs and pain medication. While "Doc" was examining him, the second one called the number on the oncologist's card. After several rings, someone picked up.

Number two held his free hand up in a gesture for silence, and said, "Hello, this is David. Please connect me with Nurse (mumble, mumble)."

"Hello, David, I hope you're feeling a little better. I'll get you Nurse Morgan, please hold."

The conversation continued with Nurse Morgan. The second stranger playing the role expertly, placing his hand over the mouthpiece to simulate poor sound quality.

After a while, he hung up, and with a smile, faced the other two and said, "Yup, he's good. Cancer, four months to live."

'Doc," taking David's head in both hands, held it up so that their eyes met. "Let me tell you about our little club. If you're lucky you can become a member. There are many advantages to joining, but the club is secret, and you will be required to keep your mouth shut and recruit an additional member. In fact, that is why you are being recruited."

David blinked several times to clear his vision. He then heard, "This is a very exclusive club whose members have been cured of the incurable."

"Doc," his new "friend" introduced him to the other two members of the club, each of whom gave him the same sad smile when asked about the cure. The story that they had told him, while at first unbelievable, made more sense on reflection.

Without going into who said what to David, the gist of the story was that a cancer-research group in Arizona had discovered that individuals with a certain cellular mutation NEVER developed any kind of cancer! Discrete attempts were made to locate an organ donor with the required mutation.

Through the organ donor program, they finally acquired an acceptable, comatose, technically alive, but legally brain dead body. First the researchers injected the body with relatively benign cancer cells (Now there's an oxymoron!). Although several times near death, it always managed a cure, and ultimately all of the cancer disappeared. Then they tried the much more virulent forms, each time with the same result—the body sickened, but then healed, eradicating each form of the disease. When, someone on the staff developed incurable cancer, possibly from some of the experiments in progress, the researchers did the obvious. Having matching blood type, they started her on blood transfusions, hoping that the magic "X" factor was in the blood. It wasn't! In desperation, they joined her to the comatose body, and then…and then…

The system that finally worked, (and it did work!), was a connection between the blood system, the lymphatic system, and a simple surgical flesh join. The rest, of course, is history—if you know where to ask the right questions! It was covered up, of course. After all, a cure had not been found, and the legal rights to the body may still rest with the surviving kin. It just would not do to tell people that old Uncle Bob would be worth millions—dead, but only slightly!

David stirred. He had been thinking about the club, "What did they do together?" He looked around at the quiet room. The wall clock indicated three and the dark said it was morning. He somehow knew that the cure was working; he was feeling much better. He thought that only three weeks like this wasn't bad. In his drugged state, he did not know that a week had already passed.

He felt a tug on his arm and heard an almost inaudible sound. Turning, he found himself looking directly at the face of Healer1066. "My God, that look of absolute torture! Was it still human?" he sub vocalized. As if in answer to the unvoiced question, its eyes opened fully, staring directly back at him with such intensity that he wanted to scream. Then it hit him! "It knew! By God, 1066 knew, but couldn't do a thing about it!" But David now knew, too. And with this knowledge he would face his remaining time, intimately linked to this *thing* that wanted to die as much as he wanted to live. How could he avoid those pleading eyes that were its last link to humanity?

He knew that if it could talk, it would say, "Please tell them to LET ME DIE." He knew that for the rest of his life he would remember that because he lived, another person would be condemned to perpetual Hell.

He had seen the pain in the other's eyes. He knew that although the Healer could no longer fully heal itself, it had healed enough so that it was a thinking and feeling being. And because of the intimate joining to the healer, the bond would remain for the rest of David's life. Now David knew that within this medically created *thing* was a tortured sole longing for release!

David did not know how he would live his new life, knowing what he now knew. And since there was no one around to say it for him, David said it for himself—"Welcome to the club."

This was his initiation!

FLASHBACKS!

I'll tell you about flashbacks. I keep mine in a box in the back of the closet underneath a pile of old clothes. The box has a lock on it, but every once in a while, in the early hours of the morning, I swear the sound of the lid opening wakes me and then.

Flash—

There he is in front of me. The doctor with the sad brown eyes. I hear again some of the words. "Cancer…radical mastectomy…chemotherapy, radiation," and finally, "hopeful results."

Again I have the dry heaves, but I do not upchuck on the bed. I am wide awake now, and I will have another memory.

It is 1960. A beautiful girl, sunlight on her hair leans against a tree. The smile says, "I have been loved, and the world is beautiful." The picture stays in my mind and in my heart. I do remember; it was our honeymoon, and I, too had been loved.

No matter how hard I try, that damn box won't stay shut. Scenes flash through my mind at the oddest times.

I picture an emaciated woman on a reclining chair with a chemotherapy drip in her arm, slowly being poisoned. I hear once again the doctor say that it would be better if she were post menopausal, but he could help that along by cutting out her ovaries. Again I see the scar where something soft and wonderful used to be. I see the burns from the radiation and visualize what the insides must look like, and then holding her close with the feel of hard chest bone underneath skin stretched taught and scarred.

Yes, she allows me close to her, and she loves me. I am the only person in the whole world that can do this, and how lucky I am that she loves me enough.

But it wasn't enough. Here it comes, the flash that I dread. She is in my arms. I hear her exhale, but it doesn't sound right. I wait for the next breath, but it never comes. The realization hits me. "NOOOOO!" I scream. The scene speeds up.

The medical technician comes to check out the crime scene. Crime scene? Yes, he consults with the doctor on the death certificate to say that she did not die by my hand. Again, the feeling of shock and revulsion that anyone would think that.

"Well," he says, "these things happen—a lot."

I have a new life now. I remarried, and my wife knows all about my past. In fact, she helped me through some rough times afterwards. I am very lucky to have found love twice in my life.

I must have left the locked box full of flashbacks in my old house because I don't see it in my closet. I try not to think much about my old life, now that I have some history with my present wife. Still, though, every so often, and sometimes when I least expect it, one of those flashbacks jumps out of nowhere to bite me.

I'm okay with it, though—after all; I'm the one still living. Aren't I?

A SMALL TOWN IN IOWA

—a town so small that even on a cloudless day, it really couldn't be seen from orbit.

In the last half of the 20th century, several high-tech space/ aircraft companies, Grumman, being one of them, actually proposed that a very large antenna be built in space to capture solar energy and beam it to earth as an alternate energy supply. Technology, it was felt, would solve all our problems. Regardless of the feasibility of the project, I felt that the potential for catastrophe was just too great. This story, written in the 1980s, involves a flawed technology. Although not the primary focus, some technical details are important to the story. Read on and see if you agree.

He looked up from his note taking, his eyes distance-focused on the Earth viewed through the station port. All of North America was cloud covered, obscuring the boundaries between land and water. His eyes scanned the land, picking out what references they could, finally settling on a patch of brown, barely discernible through the clouds. With his practiced eye, he was looking for a small Iowa town, but the clouds made identification impossible. "Well, almost impossible," he sub—vocalized, trying to convince himself that he could, indeed, see it.

His eyes moved back to the work surface.

This report was going to be difficult to write, he thought. It was important to get all the facts straight; to somehow explain the disaster that had caused the world's first solar microwave power plant to shut down. Once again, his fingers played over the keys, re-ordering his notes and displaying his latest revisions on the screen. As he reviewed what he had written, the terse sentences keyed within him a re-creation of the events, making him feel as if he were part of an old "edited for television" movie....

***

The first hint that anything was wrong was an abnormal indication on the main monitor screen. It was just a flash, a warning number, and it was not even noticed until the next shift read the computer log.

A query, requesting details, showed that one of the small computers on the great microwave array had not been able to keep up with the demands placed on it, and had reset itself.

And what were those great demands? It was simply to monitor the bending and twisting of the massive array, and to compute which local control jets should be fired to stop it.

He remembered the feeling he had when he first saw the warning. He had felt important because here was something to be looked into, something that required a human with instincts for things out of place. As he worked through the logs, he felt a kinship with the early astronauts. Part of his mind digested the data while another part put words to his feelings, sometimes feeding them to his consciousness.

"Now, those guys really knew they were important!" And, "My God, what primitive machines they had!" And, "What guts to trust their lives to machines whose programs were not capable of learning, and that had all the patched-up logic in the original code!"

He cleared his mind and settled into his task. Guided by his professional instincts and training, he began to look for the basic problem which caused the array computer to generate an alarm.

In spite of his best efforts, he could find nothing wrong! But as other problems came up, the computational overload mystery became less and less important, until it was all but forgotten, a mistake he would never be able to forgive himself for!

Time for a break, he thought; *this is getting me nowhere!*

Out in the "commons," the first person that he saw was Janet. How nice; she didn't say anything. Somehow, she always knew what he needed, and right now, it was a good cup of coffee. She took one look at him, did an about-tumble down the mainway, and came back shortly, presenting him with a hot bubbler of the brew. He accepted it graciously; the offer and thank you taking place with zero-gravity body language that had become natural to all of them. In her case, the gestures were special, as was their relationship.

An earth-bound person may have missed the subtleties of the body language, not having lived in a zero-gee environment, which allowed for a whole extension on the type of gestures. After all, if your feet are not holding you up, the way they are used certainly adds another dimension to the conversation!

As the warm coffee worked its magic on him, he relaxed a bit and attempted conversation. "Do you remember the way we first built the array, Janet?"

"I do," she said. "I also remember the great times we had, but what are you really driving at?"

"When we first laid out the array, we took three work modules, linked them with cables, and programmed each of them to keep the cables taught. That way the cables defined a perfectly flat plane to set up the array geometry."

"So?"

"Well, there were almost no control problems. I mean, how much control does it take to get three robots to keep their lines taught? Oh, sure, we asked that they not whip around too much, but it was really minimal."

Taking a guess at the source of his guilt, Janet said, "Look, the control programs were eight ways redundant. Each computer could run those calculations and still have power left over to play chess! There was no reason to suspect that they could overload—I've checked that at least ten times."

She really didn't think that her words would make him feel any better.

His face showed the distress that he was feeling. As soon as she paused, he continued. "Let me try it another way. Remember, as each section got built, we put stabilizer jets on to keep its position, and as we linked them, we also linked the sensors?"

She remembered. She remembered thinking how clever it was to be able to build a lightweight space structure and stabilize it with jets, rather than try for bigger and stronger beams. Even below, where weight was relatively cheap, one had to be careful. She had, after all, seen the disaster film of the twentieth century Tacoma Bridge collapse.

So what was he driving at? she asked herself. They had built the greatest achievement of mankind, a solar array that converted sunlight into power and beamed it to earth to the receiving plant supplying the electrical needs of much of North America.

On impulse, she maneuvered around towards the viewport, aligning herself so that she could see the large array. There it was, magnificently reflecting the sunlight from its edges, so huge when seen up close, and yet insignificant in the vastness of space. It was a perfect composition for an early Bonestell[21] painting; the eye held, attracted to the beauty, and yet in your gut, you could feel the impartial deadliness of it.

She knew that he was looking at it, too. His concentration was almost palpable; perhaps it was a pheromone that he was generating, but what she sensed was his hate of it.

His deep inhaling, turning to a sigh, broke the moment. "In spite of what you said, somehow the control programs couldn't cope. It's time to go out there and take a close look."

They had already moved out over half the distance to the plane of the array, and were now slowing, aiming for the first control-jet cluster. Regulations aside, they each knew that it was folly to free-fall without a partner, and they certainly didn't want any more disasters to happen.

They had slowed to under a meter per second and positioned themselves in a crouch to take up the landing shock—and hit together, about two meters apart, clinging to a support rail facing each other.

"Janet, look at the rail; it's bent!" "That rail should have stopped a truck! There is no way we could have bent it!"

Nevertheless, there it was, bent where they had hit it, to the point where they would have to take it inside to be straightened.

They both hung there just looking at it, she doing mental stress calculations, and he thinking of the impact on the control programs. Without saying anything, Janet positioned herself between the jet cluster and the rail. With one foot on the jets for a base, she pushed upwards against the bend. To the surprise of both of them, the rail unbent, but the jet cluster now pointed up at an angle about thirty degrees from where it originally aimed!

At this point, Janet knew what had happened! Whatever properties the structure originally had, it was no longer stable. Perhaps it was a result of prolonged microwave exposure. Perhaps the plastic just deteriorated in the direct sunlight. There were a thousand guesses and only time and analysis would pinpoint the mechanism. She could not catch his expression through the sun visor, but she knew him well enough to know that, despite his private grief, he realized the implications of her discovery. They made their way back in silence, each isolated in their own thoughts.

When they returned to the station, they separated wordlessly, but not without a parting touch, really, just a toe brush as they pushed in opposite directions.

In his own "cubie" he activated his display, selecting views of the array under constructions. His thoughts went back to the evolution of the monster, how they had developed the control theory so that small jets could control the bending. How they had developed the programs and anxiously checked them out, knowing full well that if they were flawed, they would have the world's largest structure acting like a kids' slinky toy, with the oscillations building up until it tore itself apart, taking them with it. Though nobody said it, clearly they were all worried about this possibility.

But everything worked within design limits. How bitter he felt! That anxious first phase was long behind them, and the programs worked exactly as they were designed.

No, he thought, *the problem that we left unsolved was what happens when nothing was within design limits, when all the thrust angles changed.* In fact, later investigation would show that Janet's' first guess had been the correct one. Long exposures to radiation had affected the structure, allowing the thrust angles on the small jets to change unpredictably under load.

The programs had tried their best to compensate, had tried to keep the huge power generator focused on the receiving station in Iowa; tried to keep the hundred gigawatt beam flowing into the power grid at the one point designed to receive it.

In the end, it could not do it. The undulations of the main structure were large enough to be felt and seen from the tethered maintenance station itself. Of course the main station watchdog program shut down the power generator—just as soon as the fault was detected. Every safety worked exactly as designed!

The would-be report writer looked back at the display. His hand held a printout of an e-mail that he would never send. It was addressed to his parents in a small town in Iowa. It was true that the hundred-gigawatt beam shut down when the array became unstable; in fact, the master program caught the instability the first time that it happened, just forty thousandths of a second after the event.

But the system did not shut down before the concentrated power beam had made a devastating sweep through a certain town in Iowa where his parents lived, a town so small that even on a cloudless day, it really couldn't be seen from orbit.

Note: In February 1997, a shuttle mission was flown to repair the space based Hubbell telescope that had been in space only 7 years. The insulation had been damaged from space radiation.

ONE PHOTON

Imagine, if you can, being in a losing battle and wishing to run away so far that you would never be found. Now imagine that your wish came true.

One photon!

That was what one of our sensors had picked up. One photon; a single particle of light. It had come from the South Amerind station, as if that gave it direction and meaning.

We had been in this totally empty void for probably over one thousand generations, a generation being an archaic term, being set equal to 7200 cycles of our planetime measurer. Even planetime was somehow related to one revolutions of some planet called Earth, where, so the records indicate, we had been associated with before recorded events.

The only thing known, or at least our religion tells us, was that at one time, we could look up and see an infinity of lights which was a collection of many "galaxies." Two lights were close enough that they illuminated our planet and gave warmth, and we could walk on our planets' surface. We had contact with other humans on other planets, as if such a thing was possible. The records are there, in an ancient language lost to us. Our Godstory tells us, as written in the five books of creation, that in the beginning, when we ourselves were gods, and could commerce with the other gods on other planets, we had a war which for sure, we would lose. It was then that we used our technology to reach into the forbidden space-time-volitions for a way to move our planet as far away from this conflict as possible. We committed all our resources to this task, secretly at first, because our

Godteach had forbidden it, citing many cases of foolhardy attempts which ended in the disappearance of those involved. Our God can be a vengeful God, who punishes mightily those who violate Gods laws! In the end, when we knew that our enemies were on the way to destroy us, we agreed that it was better to suffer the wrath of God, than to be killed for sure.

So we "threw the switch."

And nothing happened! That is, until we looked up and saw

NOTHING!

Not one star, not one sun; no light; NOTHING.

Where we were was not known, nor could it be known. When we were was also not known, because "when" implies some known position of suns, stars, satellites. NOTHING!

We mobilized the planet, moving underground, because the surface was growing colder by the day, day being one revolution of our planetime measurers, since we could not see if our planet revolved.

And so began the start of our recorded Godstory, when God punished us and sent us out of paradise and we were no longer gods.

One thousand generations passed, but we never gave up trying to return to paradise, or at least trying to find it. We had already insulated as much as we could of the planet to avoid heat lose, but we knew that eventually all heat would be lost, and the last consumable consumed, and all movement would slow as the temperature reached absolute zero. And at some point, life would no longer be possible.

And then, we became hopeful. We had done much and had accepted our fate, never losing faith in our God, who had brought us out of paradise to show us that He was still our God.

And so we scanned in all directions, looking for a sign, for a place to return to.

One photon!

My father told me that he was the one who had first seen the record of it. If there had been another, then we would know which way we should go. It would be simple; go toward the light, for there must have been something there to have emitted the light. Of course, one must be prepared to move when we could figure out the direction to move in.

Building the means to move our planet started with my grandparents' generation. My fathers' generation built the planet drive, knowing full well that if it were used, it would take energy from us to drive the planet, thus bringing closer the day when all life would freeze. But the opinion of the time was that it was better to die pursuing a goal, then to die anyway, living just a bit longer.

So here I wait, doing my father's old job of checking the external sensors. If we get another photon from the same direction, then we would know that the universe is "that way." But what if we get one from another direction? That could mean that we are spinning and pointing differently or perhaps that there are at least two universes. Could that mean that there are at least two Gods, each one having His own universe? I have pondered that question all my life and cannot believe other than what I have been taught. But that does not make it so: only that to me it is true.

It is not an easy thing to see the limitation of your beliefs. My mother had a simple explanation when I would ask her questions about when things go wrong for no apparent reason. She would say, "Man plans; God laughs!"

To her this was the simple answer for all things beyond her understanding. Sometimes the simplest answer is the correct one. I wish that I understood the joke.

And still, I am afraid. We cannot know how to undo what has been done, and the awesome responsibility for that decision could fall to me if another photon is detected, and I must point the direction that we would commit to. What if I would be wrong? Then we would be giving up our planet heat to move nowhere, hastening the day when we would all be frozen.

Oh, well, maybe I can be lucky; maybe we will not see another photon in my lifetime.

Then that decision can be left to my children!

THE GIFT

Children, of course, are the greatest gift of all. Out of love, we give them to ourselves.

The old man sat alone on the sand silhouetted against the red clouds of sunset. He had all the time in the world, and he would take whatever he needed. His mind expanded, allowing feeling to touch him. He had just one more thing to do before life would finally flow from him.

He had lived two hundred years, the last fifty softly and with great joy. *Most people,* he thought, *would never live long enough to develop the fine attunement to all living things that he had been allowed to enjoy.* This saddened him, but he knew that only with great age did one's mind achieve the power. This was a rather late development in the evolution of mankind, and he was one of the first. He had spent the last five years preparing for this event, the final act to give meaning to his long life, to say thanks to the world that nurtured him, and to pay his last respects.

There! He found what he was looking for; the child-mind up the beach, frightened by the sound and the fury of the waves. What potential this mind had! So young, and yet it understood the naturalness of the sea and the wind.

Still, the boy was afraid, having been abandoned by his parents in mock punishment for some small thing; that he had lingered too long, caught up in the wonder of the sand, the wind and the surf, in spite of the fear of it. And so, his parents, who deeply loved him, were deliberately showing him hurt in order to prevent the possibility of future hurt. In truth, they were angry for having to look for their son, rather than pursue their own plans.

The old man touched the young mind, soothed it and made it understand the selfish nature of love. Having done all that, without this child becoming aware of his touch, he gave the boy the power of self-confidence. And while he was at it, he gently coaxed certain thought patterns to help this very special child to never lose the sense of wonder and awe at the beauty of the universe. When he was done, the old man, exhausted from his effort, smiled with inward satisfaction.

The next day, a frail body was found on the beach. It was smiling.

Somehow it seemed right.

RAIN

It is good for many things—flowers, trees, and growing boys.

"Rain!" he said. "Why today of all days!" He normally liked the rain; it had a calming effect on him, and seemed to make him think better. But he did not like getting wet.

He re-entered the house and searched for his jacket, *Just in case,* he thought. He found it in a heap at the foot of his bed, slung it loosely over his shoulder, and went outside. His bike was propped against the house, just where he had left it. He tied his jacket around his waist, mounted his bike, and rode down the path towards the Center.

The day was hot and humid, and it felt good to pass through the air-door into the climate controlled environment that was the Center. True, if he looked up through the Lexaglass, the sky still looked threatening, but today he wouldn't notice. He quickly skirted the shopping area and entered the park-like surroundings that was the counseling area. There she was, just ahead, seated at her desk under the tree.

Joyce had been his counselor ever since he started school, from the first grade, if there had been grades. He knew that at one time school did have grades, and that everyone progressed through them according to age, rather than ability, interest, and suitability. However, all that was past history. Together, he, Joyce, and his parents had planned every phase of his learning since he first entered the system at the age of two. But now he was ten, and had all his requirements for what he wanted. Finally!

"Hi, Joyce," he said, addressing her with the easy informality that they had developed over the last eight years.

"Well, hello, Dave," she said, looking up from her work. "It's here, but I want to go over some things with you first, okay?"

Oh, boy, here it comes, he thought, knowing full well he had no choice.

"Sit down, Dave," she said.

He laid his bike down. *I'll have to fix that kickstand,* he thought to himself and seated himself on the bench, instinctively moving under the shade of the tree, in spite of the overcast sky.

"Where is it?" he wondered, half aloud.

Joyce fingered a keyboard, paused, and said, "Look at this, Dave." She was referring to a small display device showing a chart, which read:

David A. Kimball: Student
Selected Achievement Skills
Language Usage Expected: 0.39 Actual: 0.25
Math Concepts Expected: 0.45 Actual: 0.51
Suggested Study Area: Report Writing
Basis for suggestion: Develop language usage around interests
See courses:
ER 30
ER 115

—End of report—

Dave knew full well what this meant; He would have to improve his language skills by taking a report-writing course BEFORE taking the experimental logic course that he had been wanting.

"Well, Dave, you may be in luck."

"What do you mean?"

"There is a way to take the 'Logic_X1' course that you've been wanting, if you're willing to take on more work than you have been lately."

Joyce went on. "Your workload ability is higher than what you have been doing, I'm sure you realize that?"

She paused, waiting for acknowledgment. Dave thought for a moment, and then nodded.

She continued. "Since Logic_X1 is still experimental, we need feedback from it. If you are willing to take the latest version of it, I can get you credit for report writing if," she emphasized, "you critique the course as you go along. I know you hate to write, but you can use your own station and route it to me."

She paused again, waiting for a reply. When Dave said nothing, she reached into a cardboard box behind her desk and took out a white plastic-like cube and placed it between them. It was about the size of a large shoe box, and judging by the way she handled it, it was fairly light.

"Look, Dave. This is the entire course. No books, instructions or anything."

The cube really looked interesting. Dave wondered how the entire course WAS the cube. His curiosity being greater than his aversion to report writing finally forced his decision. What bothered him, though, was that she had him, and they both knew it.

"Ooo…kay!" he said. "Only, how do I do the writing?"

"Critique," she said. "I'll leave a note for you under *Assignments*."

Having put that problem off, he could now concentrate on the cube. "What do I do with it?" he asked.

"I don't know, but I'm sure you will figure it out."

He picked it up and found that it really was light. He cris-crossed the elastic straps over it, securing it to his bike rack, and started to leave.

"Dave?"

He stopped. Turning, he looked at Joyce, questioningly; she was grinning.

"Goodbye?"

"Oh, sorry. Goodbye. And thanks, I'll critique it real good."

He turned and rode away, hiding his embarrassment, and all the while aware of the back of his neck turning red. With his jacket still tied around his waist, he cleared the air door at full speed.

The drenching that he got reminded him of why he had taken his jacket, but now it was too late to do anything, like put it on to stay dry.

"Dave, is that you? Wipe your feet before you track up the rug."

"Yes, Mom," he said, allowing the door to slam as he bounded up the stairs to his room.

He made a clearing on his desk of approximately 1.05 square feet and set down the 1.00-square-foot cube. Now he could examine it more closely. It appeared to be solid white plastic with no cracks or markings.

Well, he thought, *she did say that I would figure it out.*

He picked it up, turned it over and set it down again. He did this several more times with nothing happening. Then, as he was about to turn it over yet again, he touched only the side near his right hand, on the top of the cube, in black letters appeared:

A=1

Startled, he withdrew his hand, and the writing disappeared. He touched it again.

A=1

He touched the left side.

B=1

Touching the other sides, he found he could also make the writing C=1 and D=1 appear. This was interesting, and sort of fun, but what else could it do? He picked up the cube with both hands. No writing appeared. He set it down, still holding both sides, and on top appeared:

A•B=1

He tried the other pair of sides and got C•D=1. Then it dawned on him! Touching one side AND the other side gave him the letter representing the sides with a dot between them and "=1." He thought for a moment, *Would it work for three sides?* He tried it and got; A•B•D=1, followed by A•B•C=1. Stretching both thumbs and forefingers, he touched all four sides. He got: A•B•C•D =1

THIS ENDS LESSON 1

DEMONSTRATION OF ANDING FUNCTION (.) AND = LOGICAL TRUE (.)

The cube went blank! Try as he would, he could not make it do anything again. There was only one thing to do, the thing that almost every growing ten-year-old does when confronted with a problem, and that is to raid the refrigerator! He liked the first lesson, but it left him with more questions than answers, and he didn't even know what the questions were.

That night, Dave switched on the video, selecting *keyboard control*. Typing in "ASSIGNMENTS," he read:

HI DAVE *** REQUEST REPORT WRITING; SCHOOL EDITION; LEVEL 4 *** JOYCE

He could see that this was going to take real effort!

"Oh, well." He keyed in the request to the school library, and hit the print button. It didn't look too bad, only a page and a half to read. He took it up to his bedroom, detouring past the refrigerator.

It was mid-summer now, and he was really getting into the course, that is, between baseball, swimming, and trips with his friends and family. One day he found a combination of symbols that opened the top of the cube. Inside, there appeared to be circuits with symbols and connecting lines, along with a store of spare circuits and other items.

THE NEXT DAY THE CUBE FAILED!

Well, it wasn't a real failure. It was just that, sometimes, the answers were wrong. He worked through the logic that opened the cube. Should he? *Well,* he thought, *I'd better learn a little about those symbols first.* He examined the spare parts and found a card containing the following:

MAINTENANCE= A•B•C•D• (OPEN)

Since the cube was already open, he tried sides A and B and, using both knees, D and E. Then the circuit came alive with lights! It took him almost a week before the lights began to make sense. He found that he could get different light patterns by entering different logic patterns, and the symbols on the inside were an indication of the light pattern. One light, however, he was not able to get to turn on. He thought about it a lot, and then he lost interest.

It was a rainy Sunday, and they were driving to Grandpa's house. Dave's thoughts were lazily drifting from the passing scenery to thoughts of friends. His mind was passing in and out of a dream-like state that was characterized by certain rhythmic brain patterns called (years ago) Alpha.

"Right tail-light."

"What?" Dave said suddenly, realizing that he had missed the first part of the sentence, and probably most of the monologue.

"I said," his father repeated, "we need a new right tail-light."

"Why?" Dave asked.

"Bulb's about to go."

"How can you tell?"

"The brake works the bulb just fine, but when I turn on the flasher and the brake, the flash rate slows. You can see the circuit in the maintenance manual, but the way it's hooked together, if the bulb resistance changes, so does the flash rate, and they sometimes change just before they go."

Now that was interesting to Dave! He wasn't thinking of it consciously, but he was assimilating the information that some things can work well by themselves, but not together.

When they got to his Grandparent's house, just as soon as they got past all the hugging and other "sissy" stuff, he got a pencil and paper and went to work on the troublesome circuit problem. He soon had three possible failed parts to try, and the cube contained a package of spares.

As it later turned out, he got it on the second try. It was a single circuit that required ten signals being in a particular combination to produce an output, but when a certain pattern was present, it would give a false output.

It rained for the next three days, and on the fourth day he completed the course.

As he rode towards the center, he was thinking of how to tell Joyce that the experimental cube was no good, and that he could not write a positive report (critique) on it. He would tell her, he decided, that because it was broken he had to fix it; he even had to figure out how to open it by himself.

After he told her, she seemed impressed, and even said that he could take an advanced course if he wanted, and that she would tell the manufacturer.

After Dave left, Joyce wondered about the cube failure. It wasn't every ten-year-old that could do what Dave had done: fix such a complex thing like that cube!

When Dave was well out of sight, Joyce opened her desk drawer and took out a small plastic card, which she placed on top of the cube. Instantly the face displayed the following.

STUDENT RECORD:
PERCENTAGES
LOGIC FUNDAMENTALS: 90
CIRCUIT DIAGRAMS: 95
FAILED CIRCUIT PROBLEM: SOLVED CORRECTLY AFTER 6 TRIES.
STUDENT QUALIFIES FOR ADVANCED COURSES
SATISFIES PREREQUISITES 1 THRU 6
PLEASE ENTER THIS IN STUDENT RECORDS.
REMOVING CARD AUTOMATICALLY RESETS THIS DEVICE FOR NEXT STUDENT

Joyce removed the card and logged in the required information. Then she decided to stroll over and treat herself to a double-chocolate ice cream cone. She was as proud of Dave as he himself was!

ENDNOTES

[1] Sludge stream does not quite translate correctly. The closest approximation would be "shit's creek."

[2] Gone-over refers to the people's auto-heart slowdown to prevent massive blood loss from trauma. When this happens, the muscles surrounding the blood vessels to the head compress rhythmically insuring a decreased but adequate blood flow to the brain. This single survival mechanism has allowed many of our great leaders, who tended to take too many chances, to survive and contribute to the gene pool.

[3] The author has had the opportunity to work with Dr. Lewis Smith, infrared astronomer of Earth, 1970s local calendar. He had developed a computer program that added successive infrared data so that very weak signals became visible. The technique worked so well that it captured the infra red signature from water molecules in space.

[4] Note the lower-case for individual names. Only great leaders and revered groups are capitalized to show respect.

[5] Tevlachim: A formal encounter whereby all problems between two people are reconciled, apologies made and debts paid. It begins in the old tradition, "My brother, my friend, please forgive me for the sins that I have committed against you." One is obliged to do so on the eve of the New Year.

[6] Jadrel later became of great influence; therefore I have edited these notes to capitalize his revered name.

[7] His—"His" when referring to individuals is used for convenience and does not imply that there is a "hers," since we do not differentiate into two sexes as do the animals of this world.

[8] The biggest insult that you can say is that someone is indifferent to the fate of another, just as the excretory orifice is indifferent to that which passes through it.

[9]Dung Egg—Spontaneous exclamation, refers to offspring of discarded eggs laid in pile of excrement.

[10] Viruses off the Vine?/Study: Plants may have infected animal kingdom deep in our past. AFTER CAREFULLY scrutinizing the "spelling" of various genes, researchers in Australia find that deep in the past a virus from plants found its way into animals, creating a whole new class of disease...Author Robert Cook, STAFF WRITER, Long Island, *Newsday* 8/3/1999 Page C03; "Discovery Section."

[11] Concern Over Ancient Viruses in Genes

Like timeworn baggage left over from evolutions past, some of the viruses that infected our oldest ancestors still lie embedded within humanity's genes, scientist report. Such "endogenous" viruses are generally harmless, but they do get...Author Robert Cook. STAFF WRITER Long Island Newsday, 10/5/1999 page C03, Discovery section.

[12] Lions; these creatures had developed names for the animal. This, their word, refers to a large quadruped that hunted in pairs and groups.

[13] Some NauticalTerms:

Longboat—Viking sailing vessel pointed at both ends and very seaworthy.

Mast—Vertical pole holding the sail

Line—Rope used in a boat.

Spar—Pole used to attach a sail.

Port—To the left when facing the front of the boat.

Starboard—To the right when facing the front of the boat.

Port tack—Sailing sideways to the wind which is coming from the left.

Leeward—on the downwind side.

Ship oars—Command to bring oars into the ship, and fast.

Halyard—line which pulls the sail up.

Bow—front of the boat

[14] Bell Labs: We broke data speed record: Reuters March 22, 2002, 1:50 PM PT. Bell Labs, the research arm of Lucent Technologies, said that, in a demonstration, it sent a massive 2.56 terabits of data per second over a distance of 2,500 miles, the equivalent of sending the contents of 2,560,000 novels every second across the United States. One terabit is a little over one trillion bits of data.

[15] IBM report to stockholders, March 2002, p 43, "All computers [and computer users] will join '"The grid." People will access the resources of the world…interwoven into a gigantic grid." Also, "One virtual identity—single, encompassing and under our total control." [YEAH, RIGHT!—my comment.] And only a year later. Reported in the IBM 2003 annual report on uses of their Websphere technology.

Xie Huanzhong, Director general, Department of Science and Technology, Ministry of Education, Peoples Republic of China. "Upon completion, the China Education and Research Grid will be capable of linking more than 200,000……conducting 15 trillion calculations per second."

Common Agents at the turn of the century automatically e-mailed stock conditions, weather alerts and news items being set up in a web page specific to a particular user.

[16] Not the Kevin Kelly, founder of BigBuzz Web Design.

[17] "Patterns within patterns:" although it would seem that it would lend itself to chaos analysis, it was something different. This behavior was recognized by many writers. See for example, Herbert's reference to wheels within wheels in his Dune series.

[18] Charles *Furst, Origins of the Mind,* Orienting Responses, chapter 3.

[19] *Long Island Newsday*, 7/2/2004. Scientists analyze perception of self…If you think your body ends with, well, your body…" Where you end and its corollary, where you are, is a learned thing.

[20] Man has always fought for freedom over oppression. It is ironic that this story, too, involves a battle on a more personal scale than the one that occurred in Hastings in the year 1066.

[21] Chesley Bonestell, world-renowned painter of celestial objects has inspired many people with the beauty and wonder of space.

Printed in the United States
75434LV00006B/25-33

9 781424 161638